The sheets were rumpled as Meg slipped into the bed

She sighed as Daniel slid his arm around her. And registered the fact that unconsciously, in sleep, he wanted her. That, or he was having an extremely enjoyable dream.

She snuggled closer. Kissed his neck. Breathed in the scent of him, a clean, masculine warmth. Kissed him again and grinned at the dazed expression on his face as he started to surface.

"Meg?' he said softly. In wonder, his hand drifted to her breast.

"Forget what I said earlier, Cowboy," she murmured. "A girl's allowed to change her mind...."

He groaned and reached for her.

She smiled against his mouth as she kissed him.

He slid his tongue inside her mouth and she was lost.

Her last coherent thought as he moved over her and settled his body between her thighs was that this was going to be the sweetest, hottest ride of her life....

Dear Reader,

Elda Minger is known for her sensual writing, dynamite heroes and wicked sense of humor. Little wonder her last Temptation title, *Christmas with Eve,* was nominated for a RITA by the prestigious group, Romance Writers of America. This talented author has appeared on numerous bestseller lists and also writes single titles.

Temptation turns up the heat again this month with Elda's sizzling-hot book *Night Rhythms.* Meg Prescott and Daniel Willett have their very own private sensual reunion the day she shows up in town. But is their relationship just a simple case of lust? Find out!

We hope you have been enjoying all the Blaze books. These are bold, provocative, *ultrasexy* stories guaranteed to thrill and entertain. Look for the next two Blaze titles.

**#657 *SCANDALIZED!*
Lori Foster (November 1997)**

**#666 *NIGHT HEAT*
Lyn Ellis (January 1998)**

Happy reading,

Birgit Davis-Todd
Senior Editor

Elda Minger
NIGHT RHYTHMS

Harlequin Books

TORONTO • NEW YORK • LONDON
AMSTERDAM • PARIS • SYDNEY • HAMBURG
STOCKHOLM • ATHENS • TOKYO • MILAN
MADRID • WARSAW • BUDAPEST • AUCKLAND

To Beth Wellington,
for more unselfish acts of friendship
than I care to count. You are truly one
in a million, and I'm blessed.
This one's for you.

ISBN 0-373-25749-X

NIGHT RHYTHMS

Copyright © 1997 by Elda Minger.

This edition published by arrangement with Harlequin Books S.A.

® and TM are trademarks of the publisher. Trademarks indicated with
® are registered in the United States Patent and Trademark Office, the
Canadian Trade Marks Office and in other countries.

Printed in U.S.A.

_____Prologue_____

"WOULD YOU _LOOK_ at that chandelier!"

Laura Gordon's voice dropped to a whisper as she gazed at the mass of sparkling, hanging crystals. Heather Cray almost bumped into her friend as she stared at the elegant light. Meg Prescott, bringing up the rear, her nose in the guidebook, smiled at the utter delight in her friend's voice.

The three of them had been best friends since their high-school days in Blue Spruce, Colorado. Now, since Meg lived and worked in sunny Los Angeles, Heather and Laura had scraped together some cash and flown out for a seven-day vacation blowout in the middle of February.

The gorgeous weather was reason enough. Just to get away from the cold snow, glittering ice and bitter winds of a Rocky Mountain winter was ample justification for the expense. But Meg had been determined to show her buddies a great time—and had the relentless itinerary to show for it. They'd already done Disneyland, Universal City Walk and Studios, Melrose Avenue and Malibu.

They were all getting a little tired. And punchy.

"Lots of movie stars have stayed at the bungalows of the hotel," Meg read from her marked-up guidebook. She smothered a yawn. They'd been up until almost four in the morning the night before at a blues club on Sunset Boulevard. "It says here that Laurence Olivier and Vivien Leigh hid out here. Elizabeth Taylor, too—"

"God, I just love this!" Laura motioned toward an Oriental vase on a sleek black pedestal. She pushed a strand of her unruly red hair off her forehead, then rummaged in her bag for her camera. "Meg, get over there. I want you in the picture."

Meg gave Heather the guidebook, then complied. Dressed in faded-jean cutoffs, a loud, red-and-white Hawaiian shirt and bright red thongs, she knew the contrast of her casual clothing with the simple lines of the expensive Ming vase would make for a hysterical vacation shot.

Laura snapped several pictures quickly with her small, automatic camera. Totally unselfconscious about playing the typical tourist in such elegant surroundings, she lined up both Heather and Meg against an antique chaise longue. And of course, Laura insisted on several shots of Meg beneath that stunning chandelier.

Outside, she took photos of the huge, glittering turquoise pool, the cabanas, the bar. Heather, with her sleekly bobbed brown hair and calm gray eyes, probably looked the most born to the manor of the three of them. Laura didn't pose for many pictures, but insisted on setting them up and taking them.

Palm trees ringed the opulent grounds, adding to the fantasy element. Lush emerald lawns complemented brilliantly colored tropical flowers, which filled the air with their scent. Birds twittered, plump bees hummed.

Meg, glancing around, couldn't believe they were in the middle of Los Angeles. Beverly Hills, actually. The hotel was like a sparkling oasis in the middle of the desert city.

"Boy, this is the life," Laura said, a touch of reverence in her voice, her green eyes shining. "What I wouldn't give to be filthy rich!"

"Hey, there's a guest robe on that chair," Heather whispered, nudging Meg.

It was just one of those days. They'd been laughing and singing throughout the morning, trading quips, daring each other. Not getting any sleep, relying on coffee and vacation energy—simply relentlessly intent on having a great time.

Meg was in just the mood to do something crazy—like slip into that robe, for a really classic shot. They would laugh about this one for years to come.

"Put it on, Meg," Laura dared.

Never one to step down from a dare, Meg glanced around. The pool wasn't crowded. Some guest had obviously forgotten his robe—and left an empty martini glass.

"Do it," Heather whispered.

Some little devil made her grab the plush robe, then pull it on, effectively covering her shorts and shirt. Only her toenails, painted bright, fire-engine red, peeked from beneath the white terry-cloth hem.

At least they matched her thongs.

"Slip those things off," Laura said, already composing the shot.

"Yes, Mr. De Mille." She tossed her thongs to Heather, who caught them, then doubled over with laughter.

"And pick up...pick up the glass," Heather said, then continued to laugh as Laura lined up the shot. "This is just too good!"

Meg lounged back on the chaise as if she didn't have a care in the world and flashed them both a brilliant smile. She lifted the martini glass in a classic salute to the good life, ran her fingers through her short, tousled blond hair, then grinned straight at the camera, cocking one eyebrow as if to say, "Are we having fun yet?"

And had absolutely no idea how that particular photo would come back to haunt her....

1

A mere three years and four months later...

DUFFY'S TAVERN WAS rocking.

The small bar smelled of beer and barbecue. Friday was sparerib-soup night, and even with the place booked for a ten-year high-school reunion, Bill Duffy didn't change his schedule—or his unique menu—for anyone.

There hadn't even been a contest as to where the Friday-night reunion kickoff should be held. Duffy's was the place. In the small town of Blue Spruce, Colorado, this was as close to a teen hangout as it got.

Meg Prescott opened the door and the heavy, stinging scent of cigarette smoke hit her full force. She was used to the nonsmoking, health-conscious restaurants in the City of Angels, but Duffy's was home. Memories assailed her, most of them happy.

She frowned. Both Heather and Laura had been acting squirrelly tonight, which in itself wasn't that unusual—but something was amiss. They'd sounded so strange when she'd talked to them on the phone from her hotel room. It was rare when she didn't trust her instincts, and something was telling her to be...cautious. Careful.

All three of them had always been incredible practical jokers. Their high-school teachers had literally lived in terror of what they might cook up. Meg could have sworn she heard an audible sigh of relief when the three of them had marched up to get their diplomas ten summers ago.

Now she wondered if they'd cooked up anything special for her tonight. It would be just like the two of them. Nothing mean, or truly damaging. Just something they could laugh about years later. Like that vacation. And those pictures.

Meg's lips curved into a soft smile as she surveyed the room. Laura had sent her a ton of photos from that frantic, fun-filled week in southern California. She'd laughed as she'd viewed them, especially the shots from the Beverly Hills Hotel. She'd even tacked a few up on her bulletin board, above her computer.

Now, as she surveyed the interior of Duffy's Tavern, she realized that everyone in the room was surveying her.

Immediately she did a swift inventory. Her slip couldn't be showing because she was wearing tight black jeans, a black tank top, and black boots. Sort of a Linda Hamilton-in-*Terminator 2* look. Time to kick some butt. Bad girl, big time. Mischief maker supremo.

Dark glasses suited the look, but definitely would have been overkill in the dimly lit lakeside bar. She'd wanted to look terrific tonight, getting back together with all her classmates. She'd wanted the confidence of looking good, because deep inside she really wasn't feeling that hot.

By Blue Spruce standards, she was a huge success. Because she'd left and sold a book. One novel published, and who knew how many more on the way? She was the only person here who knew she hadn't been able to even give away the other two, and that deep inside she didn't feel as if her life since graduating had added up to much.

Mother would have loved this. When Meg thought of Antonia Prescott, it wasn't with pleasure. Her mother had always held her to incredible standards, and told her, over and over, that she was different from the people of Blue Spruce. Better. Meg had often thought of telling her mother that both the American and French revolutions had happened over two hundred years ago. The "ruling class" was a thing of the past. A dead concept.

Their time spent in the "deadbeat town" of Blue Spruce had been beyond her control, her mother had repeatedly told Meg. Antonia Prescott had always made it clear that she hadn't been down on her luck when she'd crash-landed in this small Colorado town, her daughter in tow. She simply hadn't been financially able to move on to a ritzier, more upscale locale.

Their used BMW had literally run out of gas, and Antonia had, too. They'd stopped in Blue Spruce because Meg's mother had needed the time to heal from her latest divorce. But as soon as she found herself another wealthy man to marry, she'd lit out for Manhattan. "Civilization," as she'd so rudely—and publicly—put it.

Now, back in Blue Spruce, standing in the doorway of Duffy's Tavern, Meg could only hope that most of her classmates had long forgotten her mother's condescending ways. Small towns could have long memories....

Suddenly nervous, Meg ran a hand through her short, blond hair. The colorist had cost the earth, but it had been worth it because the sunny streaks didn't look like they came out of a bottle, but like she spent her days lazing away on Malibu beach with the "Baywatch" babes.

She tugged on her ear, still nervous, touching the diamond earring in her left lobe. The half-karat diamond studs had been the only killer extravagance she'd given herself when her first book was published, and they looked to be the last. Her writing career hadn't exactly taken off in the last three years.

And she was scared. She'd gambled big time, packing up her secondhand Jeep with everything she owned, including two tabby cats and Sluggo, her mixed-breed pug-and-something. She'd driven out to Los Angeles and played for the biggest stakes of all, a career in the arts. And even though she'd published a novel—achieved the dream so many people struggled for—she couldn't seem to get the rest of her career off the ground.

But no one here needed to know that. She could smile and nod and listen to other people's stories. She could modestly say *Yes, I sold a book,* and hope to God no one was genuinely interested in when the next one would come out.

It would be easy, she told herself, forcing her hand down to her side, consciously telling herself not to play with her earrings or her hair. Nervous habits. *Calm.*

Stay calm. She took a deep, centering breath and almost choked on the heavy smoke.

SHE LOOKED ABSOLUTELY adorable. And gorgeous.

Daniel Willett stayed in the shadows of the bar, peering through the bluish haze of cigarette smoke as he studied Meg Prescott. She was the only reason he'd come to Duffy's tonight, as technically he wasn't a part of this particular high-school-class reunion.

He'd graduated two years earlier, then gone straight back to his father's farm and worked for years and years. Still worked there. Still lived there. Didn't have many stories to tell, adventures to share, but he'd survived and that was good enough.

He'd wanted to see Meg again. One more time. Enough to see if he still had that incredible knee-jerk, kick-in-the-gut reaction to her sunny smile. And that incredible laugh. She'd never learned to tame it, to make it ladylike. It came barreling straight up from her belly, and he loved it. Hearing it in the hallway between classes had always made him smile.

And she'd always been laughing. In the middle of one practical joke or another. Daring. Carefree. When she'd graduated, folks around town had merely shaken their heads and wondered if the world was ready for Meg. She hadn't stayed in Blue Spruce long; she'd packed up that Jeep of hers, animals and all, and headed west for fame and fortune.

Which she'd apparently found in spades.

He'd heard the rumors. Heard of some photos circulating around town. He'd even wanted to see them, but with the ranch keeping him so busy, he'd never had a chance. And he'd been happy for her, really happy. If anyone had deserved success, Meg had. She had heart, coming back to Blue Spruce when a lot of successful people would have thought a ten-year reunion in a small town was unworthy of their time and effort.

But not Meg. She'd always been different. And in his estimation, special.

Not that he'd been able to tell her. Oh, no. He'd never been a particularly social animal. More of a loner. He'd had deep feelings for her, but he'd kept them to himself. When his younger brother, Alec, had started dating her during Daniel's junior year, it had almost killed him. Everyone in the family had loved her, even his mother, which was decidedly unusual.

Meg and Alec had gone together, on and off, for almost two years. Over that agonizingly long time, he'd watched them flirt and laugh, sneak out to the barn for a kiss and possibly more. It had hurt like hell, but he'd loved them both. He'd simply watched. And waited.

She'd won a short-story contest during the spring of her junior year, in a national magazine for teenagers. First prize. Five hundred dollars and publication in the fall issue. It had been the biggest news to hit Blue Spruce since Jake Bodine's wife Martha swore she'd been abducted by aliens. And at that moment, Daniel had realized that even though Meg and Alec had gone through an amicable breakup, Daniel would never be able to have her.

Because she was one of those people who belonged to the world.

He'd seen her at the feed store in town, talking to

someone out front, two days before she'd left. And he'd stopped to have a word with her, listened as she spun her dreams. Tipped his hat to her. Relished those few, chance moments. And remembered every single second.

She'd asked him about his dreams. Funny how no one had ever done that but Meg. Everyone else had simply assumed he was happy, working the spread his father had left the family.

And the most amazing thing was, he'd told her. About the Arabian horses. How he loved the breed, and would be happy if he could have two or three on the farm. If all he could do was watch them run out in the pasture—those delicate, powerful necks arched, those exquisite hooves pawing the ground—he would die a happy man.

She'd smiled up at him with those beautiful blue eyes, eyes a man could get lost in. Eyes that could haunt a man for the rest of his life. And she'd touched his arm, and told him she hoped that life would give him every dream he ever asked for.

Then she'd left.

He'd taken a long walk that day, with only the dogs for company. And he'd looked at the mountains, trying to find some inner peace, and wondered why he hadn't had the courage to tell her how he felt about her. The pain around his heart had been overwhelming.

But he'd known. Even as he'd formulated the question in his mind, he'd realized the truth. He had no right to her. She was so full of life, of dreams, of promise and talent. He couldn't have asked her to be a rancher's wife. Those hands, those clever hands with their slender, artist's fingers, would have grown red and chapped and blistered. She would have tried to write in her spare time—what little she would have had—and the books would never have been written.

Later at the feed store, he'd heard of her success. She'd actually sold a book. And he'd taken valuable time away from the ranch to drive two and a half hours into Denver and scout out a bookstore. He'd walked inside, feeling totally out of place—a rough, common cowboy among slick young urban professionals. Even though he read constantly, he bought most of his reading material by mail, and he hadn't felt at home in this bookstore with its enormously elaborate coffee bar, the smells of steamed milk and cinnamon, the glossy displays.

He'd found her novel, studied the picture on the flyleaf. She'd been holding Sluggo, possibly the ugliest dog in the entire world, with his funny little smashed-in pug face. He'd bought the book and taken it home, handling it as if it was crafted from solid gold bullion. He'd read it over so many times he'd lost count, and had been deeply moved.

And he'd wondered at how much Meg really saw with those blue, blue eyes.

The novel had been about a tragic ranching dynasty. Four brothers, a sister, an overbearing, controlling mother and a compassionate, dying father. The character she'd named Matthew, the oldest son, had sacrificed his life for his remaining family. He'd done what he thought was right and made peace with his soul. He'd transcended it all and found his final dream. Powerful, moving words. Vivid emotional pictures.

He'd been overwhelmed by that novel, then wondered if his own imagination had been playing tricks on him. Yet he thought he'd seen bits of himself and his brothers, Alec, Brett and Joe. The ranch, the dogs and horses. The smells, the sounds. The backbreaking, soul-destroying work. The mountains and the way the land became a part of a man's soul. The loneliness. The emptiness and quiet despair.

And in the end, the faith that sustained.

Ah, but the emotions. That was where she was truly gifted. Those people had come alive, had leaped off those pages and made him really care what had happened to them. And he'd known then, when he closed the book, put it on the side table and reached down to scratch Hunter's ears, that he'd done the right thing.

Letting her go had been the hardest thing he'd ever done. But he'd made his own kind of peace with it. And if he wanted to come to Duffy's, have a few beers and take a look at what she'd become, then that was all right.

He was so damn proud of her. And he would just have to continue to live with the choices he'd made.

"MEG! I CAN'T BELIEVE you're here!" A chunky blond woman with overprocessed hair came barreling up. Meg quickly scanned her name tag, saw the boldly scrawled "Susie" in black marker, and recognized Susie Landor, who had sat behind her in home ec and beside her in the school choir.

"Susie! It's so good to see you!" And it was. They'd shared a lot of laughs in both classes, some of the best being the time Meg had slipped lemon Joy dishwash-

ing soap into Trudy Harris's blueberry-muffin batter. It
had been an afternoon Mrs. Hecht hadn't soon forgotten.

"Now, you've got to get a name tag—" Susie began,
and Meg remembered that this woman's name had
been prominent on the form she'd filled out and
mailed in almost six months before arriving in Blue
Spruce.

"I can't believe how well you organized all this."

Susie beamed. "Kev and I wanted to get the whole
gang together. We really did have such good times—"

"You and Kevin?" Meg searched for a name, and
blessedly, it came to her. "Kevin Brackman?"

"I'm Susie Brackman now."

"I love it! The two of you used to fight all the time."

"Still do. Keeps us young." Susie steered Meg toward the back of the bar, where a portly, slightly bald-
ing man sat in one of the red vinyl booths. He had a
computer-generated list in front of him, along with a
box of name badges.

"Kev!" Susie seemed as if she were about to explode
with excitement. "Look who's here!"

"I'll be damned." Kevin stood, extended his hand
and gave Meg a warm handshake. Then he grinned
and pulled her into a heartfelt hug. "I really didn't
think you'd show."

"Why not?" Meg accepted the badge Susie handed
her, then started to laugh at the picture. Senior year she
hadn't taken the best photo. All long straight hair and
starry eyes, and a loopy grin. She looked so very
young.

"Well, you know, I mean—" Susie seemed flustered,

then recovered. "I mean, the life you live out there in California—"

"Oh, yeah. Me and my big mansion."

Susie looked at her husband, delight evident in her expression. Then she glanced back at Meg. "You know, it's great that you can just joke about it like that. I'm so glad—I mean, when I heard—I thought you'd be all changed—"

"Naw. Not me." Meg assumed she had to be talking about the book sale. Strange, how the people around you changed when you sold a novel. A lot of them had been waiting, fully expecting her to turn into a god-awful snob. A real bitch. That was one thing she was determined to never let happen. She'd had enough exposure to that kind of attitude living with her mother.

Then there were the ones who freaked out because they thought you made millions of dollars on your first sale. Unfortunately, that was another totally delusional fantasy. If only it were true, she wouldn't be half as nervous about her future as she was right now.

"Hey," she said, smiling at both Kevin and Susie. "I put on my pants one leg at a time, just like anyone else."

Susie laughed at that, Meg pinned on her badge, and the reunion officially began.

"SHE'S GONNA KILL US," Laura muttered, staring through the windshield at the neon sign outside that winked Duffy's—Duffy's—Duffy's in bold red script.

"She'll understand," Heather said, but didn't sound as sure as she should have.

"She'll never, ever forgive us," Laura replied.

"Well, what are we gonna do, sit out here all night?"

"Danielle Steel," Laura muttered again, then laughed. "Danielle frigging Steel. Me and my big fat mouth."

Heather took a deep breath, then unlocked the passenger-side door of the Toyota Celica. She hesitated as she gripped the handle. "It just kinda got out of control, that's all."

Both women were silent for a long moment.

Laura spoke up first. "But it's her life, Heather. Maybe she won't think it's that funny."

"Naw. Meg will. She loves a good practical joke." But Heather spoke without conviction.

Laura opened the driver's-side door. "We'd just better face it. I don't think tonight's a night any of us will forget anytime soon."

MEG BELLIED UP to the bar, ordered a beer, turned, and saw him walking toward her. Absolute, unadulterated delight shot through her as Daniel Willett sat down next to her. She smiled up into his gray eyes.

"Hello, Cowboy." The nickname had always been deeply affectionate.

"Hey, Baby Blue," said Daniel.

He looked good. Those gray eyes had always been sharp. Wary. As if he didn't expect good things to happen. But tonight she noticed a basic kindness within their depths.

She'd always liked him. So very much.

He was glad to see her, and that pleased her. She'd had a secret crush on him since she was thirteen, but had always thought he considered her something of a nuisance. She'd dated his brother Alec on and off for two years in high school. As much as she hated to admit it, she knew her interest in Alec had had a lot to do with wanting to get closer to Daniel.

She'd wanted to see his world, figure out what it was that made him hop on the school bus so quickly after classes were finished and, later, to trade that bus ride for his own battered red pickup truck.

His skin was weathered; he was an outdoor man. But on him, it was sexy. He had crinkly smile lines around his eyes, like a young Robert Redford. Dark brown hair. Six feet and then some. "Tall, dark and handsome" fit him to a T. He was dressed in jeans and a navy shirt.

He'd never looked better.

"Did you ever get those horses?"

She saw the deep pleasure in his eyes when she asked that question, and was glad she had. He reached for his wallet, withdrew a few pictures. He handed them to her, and the Arabian horses she saw posing in those photos took her breath away.

"Oh, my God," she breathed. "They're beautiful."

He didn't say anything. He didn't have to.

She studied them for long moments. The proud arch of their necks, the set of their tails. The shining equine intelligence in their large eyes.

"You must be so proud," she said, carefully handing them back to him.

"I am. And I'm proud of you, too."

"Oh." She felt flustered. A fraud. A woman who couldn't unload her second novel pretending she was a real writer instead of a one-book wonder. "You needn't be."

"I am. We all are."

"Thanks." She looked away, suddenly self-conscious, and fiddled with her beer bottle.

The silence grew uncomfortable.

"How's your mother?" she asked impulsively, for want of anything better to say. She hadn't really cared for Erna Willett. The woman had possessed a mean spirit. She'd driven her sons relentlessly, driven three of them right off the ranch. Always bitter, she'd worked them like pack mules, offering them little in the way of nurturing in return.

"She passed away a few years back."

"I'm sorry to hear that." The words stuck in her throat, not totally true.

"It was time."

How like Daniel. That rugged acceptance. That strength in the face of events that would have put a lesser man into the ground.

"And Brett?" This was safe territory, talking about his brothers. He'd genuinely loved them all. When they hadn't found familial companionship with their mother, the Willett boys had banded together.

"A pilot. He flies out of Denver. Comes out to see me once in a while."

"That's great!" Brett had been the baby of the family and something of a daredevil. "Joe?"

"Married and a family. Two little girls. Lives in New Mexico. Works in computers."

"He always was fascinated by them. What about Alec?"

"He's engaged to a girl from Atlanta. They live in Flagstaff."

She sensed he was watching her reaction carefully.

"That's terrific."

"No regrets?" Now he was smiling down at her.

"Alec? Me and Alec?" She laughed then, and watched those deep gray eyes light with pleasure. "Naw. We were on and off for most of those two years. I think we would've killed each other if we'd tried for something more permanent." She smiled at those memories. "Though I had this weird fantasy of becoming a member of your family. I wanted to move in, like Wendy with the lost boys, and bake you all a cake or something."

"I would have liked that."

She realized he wasn't teasing. And suddenly her heart was in her throat and she didn't know what to do.

He saved the conversation.

"I read your book."

"You did?" The thought brought her enormous pleasure.

"I even read parts of it out loud to Hunter." She must have looked as puzzled as she felt, because he explained. "My dog. She's a shepherd mix. Hunts everything and anything." He cleared his throat, and she sensed he was suddenly self-conscious, as well. "You did a beautiful job with those people."

Emotions she couldn't quite define flooded her. "Thanks. I loved those characters. I loved that story."

"Characters. That's what I meant. Not people." He

laughed then, again slightly self-conscious. "But...they seemed like real people to me."

She touched his arm. "No, I understand. I know exactly what you mean—"

"Meg Prescott! Va-va-voom, would you look at the little lady from L.A.! Gimme a kiss."

Arms engulfed her and before she knew what was happening, a warm, enthusiastic kiss was planted squarely on her surprised mouth. She almost fell off the barstool, but felt Daniel's large hand on the small of her back, steadying her.

"What!" She came scrambling up for air, then started to laugh. "Bruno, you idiot!"

Bruno Delgado weighed in at close to two hundred and fifty pounds. He still wore his long black hair in a ponytail, still wore faded jeans slung low on his hips with his beer belly protruding over them, still favored T-shirts with things like skulls, knives and motorcycle emblems on them. His favorite mode of transportation was his Harley.

She adored him.

"Hey, we didn't even think you'd make it, what with that sweet deal you have out west! How could you tear yourself away?"

She thought of the small, stucco, one-bedroom apartment she rented on Laurel in West Hollywood, and almost laughed out loud. People thought the strangest things when you sold a novel.

"Oh, come on, Bruno, what deal? I'm just like anyone else—"

"Like anyone else!" Bruno caught Bill Duffy's eye and motioned him over. "What do you guys want?"

Meg felt Daniel's firm touch on the small of her back, steadying her on the barstool. She was glad he hadn't taken his hand away. She liked the way he touched her, the way his hand felt.

"Another beer?" she said.

"Same for me," Daniel said.

"Tequila!" Bruno boomed, then turned his infectious grin on the two of them. "Say, Meg, if I take my hog out your way, can I stay at your mansion?"

"My what?"

"Your mansion. You know, the one in the pictures."

She didn't understand.

Bruno smiled at her blank expression, then snapped his fingers beneath her nose. "Hel-*lo-o!* The pool. The chandelier. The gardens. You know."

She reached blindly behind her, for Daniel's hand. His fingers closed around hers, hard and warm and callused.

"My mansion."

"Yeah. The one in 'Beverly Hills 90210.'"

When Bill Duffy set Bruno's shot of tequila in front of him, Meg reached for it with her free hand and slammed it back. She set the shot glass on the bar, then swiveled on the stool, still holding on to Daniel like a lifeline, and scanned the entire bar.

Heather and Laura were in one corner, eyeing her with apprehension. Heather, her expression worried, was dressed in shorts and a peach tank top. Laura, with her long red hair pulled up in a high ponytail, wore tight faded jeans and a lime-green crop top.

Heather raised her hand and gave Meg a tiny wave,

her fingers barely wiggling. Both of them looked guilty as hell.

"Gentlemen," Meg said, her temper nearing flashpoint. "Would you excuse me a moment? I have to go talk to my friends."

THEY HAD THEIR LITTLE powwow in the handicapped stall at the far end of the ladies' room.

"Meg, we're so sorry." Laura was genuinely contrite. She and Heather stood by the stall door, while Meg sat on the closed-lidded toilet, elbows on knees, her face in her hands.

"Oh, no." Her voice came out muffled through her fingers. "I can't go out there, I can't face those people, I can't—"

The bathroom door opened noisily and they all fell silent.

"I can't believe her!" The female voice was high and indignant. "She comes waltzing back to Blue Spruce, Miss La-Di-Da L.A. No husband, no kids, not a care in the world, no one she has to take care of or answer to. And all that stinking money. I hate her!"

"Paula, shut up!"

"Well, I do! Jeez, Al and I will be clipping coupons till we're in an old-age home, and she'll be on the French Riviera with some twenty-year-old stud—"

"Get over it! How do you know she's happy?"

"Oh, get real! All that money and she's not?"

Inside the stall, Meg simply eyed Heather and Laura. They dropped their gazes, ashamed, while Meg closed her **eyes** and felt her stomach clench.

Paula McCutcheon, her nemesis. The gods had

played a wacky little trick on Meg each of her high-school years. She and Paula had somehow always landed in the same English class—which was no mean feat, as Paula had been held behind two years running and Meg had been bumped up one. And somehow, she'd always seemed to make Paula look bad.

The woman could barely read, and had shown undisguised contempt for anything on a printed page. The fact that Meg had loved words, had excelled in English composition, had convinced Paula early on that Meg had it easy and never had to work like normal people. Meg's mother had, of course, encouraged this perception.

Meg covered her closed eyes with a hand, wondering how to keep her emotions from escalating. If only Paula knew the various jobs she'd held in Los Angeles. Waitress. A salesclerk in a bookstore. Bartending. She'd even done a few years as a clown at children's parties in Beverly Hills.

But Paula wouldn't believe her. She was too completely stuck in her own worldview.

Meg listened as Paula and her friend talked. They noisily opened their compacts, redid their faces, reveled in the gossip. Finally they finished and headed out to the bar, leaving the washroom in blessed silence.

After another short silence, Meg finally opened her eyes and glanced up at her friends.

"Money does really crazy things to people," she whispered. "It was bad enough when a lot of people only suspected I had a fortune."

"Meg, listen to me," Laura began. "It started as a kind of joke. I took the pictures to the salon the day I came back to work and showed them around. Minnie the manicurist asked if the hotel was your house, and I told her no the first few times. But it was like she *wanted* to believe it."

"She's telling the truth. Honest." Now Heather joined in, looking sick with anxiety. "By the time Laura got done showing the pictures of our vacation around, it was like they made up the story themselves."

"Totally out of control—"

"They like to think of you out there in L.A.—"

"Servants and a big-screen TV—"

"Your own bar by that pool—"

"Parties with Tom Cruise—"

"Tom Cruise?" Meg's head came up on that one, then she lowered it into her hands again with a groan of true despair.

"And...and Sting. Uh, I met Sting." Heather's voice was hushed. Scared. Meg thought they were like two little kids who knew they were in for severe punishment.

"Who else?"

"Arnold. And Bruce and Sly and Demi. At Planet Hollywood in...Vegas."

"Vegas? *Las* Vegas?"

Silence.

"What, Elvis didn't join us? Don't tell me you guys started running out of gas at this point!" She knew she was being hard on both of them, but she had to know the entire truth before she could go back out among her classmates again and feel safe.

Laura took a deep breath, then hung her head.

"Okay. Okay." She took another breath. "Okay, this is the part where the story gets a little out of control."

"I can't wait."

"You flew us out—"

"To Vegas?"

"To Vegas. For a premiere. Uh, Sly sent you the tickets 'cause he'd read your novel and wanted to option it for a movie—"

"*Sylvester Stallone* wanted to play Matthew? My Matthew? A cowboy in Colorado—" Now she was truly speechless. And mad. But she swallowed her anger. "Go on."

"Okay. Like I said, you flew us out—"

"In my own Learjet, right?"

"No, we're not that stupid!"

She stared at them, long and hard. They both glanced away—one up at the ceiling, one down at the floor.

"I said...we said...you borrowed Arnold's."

"Oh, my God." It might have been funny if it hadn't been her life they were talking about. Now she felt like more of a fraud than ever.

"I've got to get out of here," Meg muttered, running her hands through her hair in an agitated manner. She knew, what with all the styling gel she'd used and the way she was nervously sweating, that it would probably stick up in funny little clumps all over her head. But right now, her appearance was the least of her worries.

"No, wait, you can't leave yet—"

"I'm outta here." She swung open the stall door and

strode out of the washroom. Wisely, her two friends chose not to follow her.

DANIEL HAD WATCHED her enter the ladies' room with her friends, and saw how she looked when she left it. He recognized desperation on her face, plain and simple. Meg's face had always been easy to read, and tonight was no exception.

He strode toward her, intent on finding out what had her so upset. Out of the corner of his eye, he saw two more people swiftly approaching her. Both female, one had a rather hard, angry glint in her eyes.

Meg saw them at the same time, and her face paled. Then she turned and caught sight of him with obvious relief. Before he knew what she intended to do, she ran right up to him, jumped, and wrapped her arms and legs around his body.

"Cowboy, get me out of here," she whispered into his ear, an edge of panic in her voice.

"Yes, ma'am," he said, his arms tightening around her. Without looking back, he headed toward the door and out into the summer night.

2

"I AM," MEG ANNOUNCED, lying on her back in the truck bed of Daniel's new black pickup and looking up at the star-filled sky, "a total failure."

Wisely, Daniel said nothing. He sensed she needed to talk, and he was more than willing to listen.

He knew it had something to do with Paula Mc-Cutcheon. Daniel only vaguely remembered the woman from high school. Large-boned, heavyset, with dark hair and an even darker attitude. She'd been a bully then, and it seemed she still chose to operate that way.

But he didn't want to think about Paula now. He was with Meg, and that was what mattered.

They'd headed out of Duffy's, found his truck, and had been roaring out of the parking lot when Bruno had waylaid them, flagging them down with a bottle of very fine tequila. He'd handed it to Meg.

"Nothing a bottle of this won't cure." Then he'd given them both a sly look and headed back inside, his belly jiggling.

Now that same bottle, minus a couple of healthy shots, sat between them. Daniel lay stretched out on his side. He'd spread two thick sleeping bags out, and they lay on top of the densely padded material.

He wasn't quite sure what was going on, but he

could have listened to her forever. Time alone with Meg, outside the confines and structure of the class reunion, was something he hadn't counted on.

"A failure," she muttered, and reached for the bottle again. Daniel subtly bumped it out of her reach. The Meg he'd known had never been a boozer. He didn't think she'd picked up any bad habits in Los Angeles. It had to be the stress of the moment. Something had happened tonight—something that had come to a head in that ladies' room.

She would tell him in time. Friends, they'd always been able to talk to each other about anything—except his feelings for her.

He didn't try to touch her, didn't try to get close in any way. He sensed she just needed to vent, to let out some pent-up feelings, and he'd always treasured the fact that she felt safe enough with him to talk really openly. Not the superficial exchanges he participated in when he went into town for supplies. Meg always went straight to the point. She went deep.

"Failure." She hiccuped and closed her eyes. "And it's spelled *M-E-G.*"

"No one could be a failure after writing a first novel like that."

She hiccuped again, then tried to sit up and fell over against his shoulder. "Tell that to my publishers." She started to laugh. "You could call them up."

He cradled her against his side, his hands gentle. He sensed she was in a lot of pain, and decided he would get to the bottom of it.

"What happened?"

"Where?"

"Tonight. You were having a good time and all of a sudden the joy went out of the evening for you."

She didn't answer. He could feel her hesitation.

"Meg? Was it something that happened in the washroom?"

"Oh, yeah."

"Want to talk about it?"

"Too embarrassing." She closed her eyes and leaned more heavily against him. "This is nice."

His thoughts exactly. Only he would have had her wanting to be with him, not a little smashed on tequila, and the two of them ready to head on home. He'd always pictured Meg at his ranch, even though he'd known it could never happen.

"They're not bad people," he said, referring to the reunion.

"Oh, no, it's not that. I was having a great time. It's just that I don't like to tell lies."

"Like what?" Now he was intrigued.

"Like I'm this big success."

It kept coming back to that. Success or failure. Daniel knew enough about Meg's mother to know the woman's presence still lived inside Meg's head, still pushing and punishing her relentlessly. But tonight something else was weighing very heavily on Meg's mind. And he wanted to help her.

"But you are a success. That was a damn fine book."

"It was just an eensy-weensy fluke."

He thought about that for a moment, then sat up, taking her with him, steadying her with a strong arm around her shoulders. Their backs against the truck's cab, they both looked up at the stars. After a moment, Daniel spoke.

"You know, there's success on two levels. One is what other people think of you. The other is what you think of yourself. Forget about all the others, Meg. What do you think?"

She sighed, and it seemed to him she was emotionally exhausted.

"I used to think...if I just sold the one, everything would be okay. Then...it all started to fall apart."

He remained silent.

"Then I come back here, and I think to myself, look at all my classmates and the success they've made of their lives. They're married, have babies, a home. And I have...nothing."

"There's no guy out there waiting for you?" He didn't like to pry, especially when she was this vulnerable. It was definitely taking unfair advantage. But he had to know.

"Nope. Zero. A big fat zero in that department, too."

He couldn't imagine that was true. "You're being too hard on yourself." He thought of Meg's mother, and wished she'd been a little more conscious of the legacy she'd left her daughter.

"Oh, I think not." She turned to face him, and even with those spectacular blue eyes a little unfocused, she was beautiful in the moonlight. He'd parked his pickup at the edge of the lake, a lake they'd all swum in as children dozens of times. The mountains remained dark and silent in the distance. Stars blazed in the night sky.

He'd picked a secluded spot, on the far side of the

highway. He didn't want anyone to invade their privacy, take away this moment, this evening that might be all they would have together for the next ten years.

And he sure didn't want to think about her leaving again.

"You are, Meg. Way too hard." He paused, trying to find the right words. He was a man who didn't really talk a lot, but when he did he chose his words carefully.

"You can't know what's going on in their lives from the outside, Meg. They're the only ones who do. Marriage doesn't guarantee happiness. Neither does having children. Or even the greatest job in the world. I think it's a little more elusive than that."

"Were you happy, Daniel? Back in high school? Getting on that bus every afternoon at three? Never staying after to play sports or work on the school paper?"

"I...I had to make a choice, Meg. I was the oldest, and Dad wasn't well."

"And you sacrificed so your brothers could have a normal life. So they could go on and do whatever it was they wanted, so they wouldn't have to be ranchers." Her voice dropped to a whisper. "So they could get away from your mother."

The silence stretched between them.

"I was older than Alec," he said, as if that was enough explanation for what he had done.

"Only one year." Then she waited, willing him to tell her the truth.

"Yeah," he finally whispered. "I did it for them."

Now, even slightly smashed, she was focused on

him intently. He couldn't have taken his eyes off her if he'd tried.

"I always wanted to know all about you, Cowboy. I thought about you a lot when we were in school. Why you left so early. What you did. What you thought—"

"Meg—"

"What you felt. What you wanted and needed."

"Meg, don't—"

"When I wrote about Matthew, when I created him, I didn't know it at the time, but I think I was trying to figure it all out—"

He'd known. He'd known it by page thirty—that she'd taken a part of him, his heart, and put it within the pages of her novel. It should have infuriated him, but it hadn't. There wasn't much Meg could do to make him mad.

"I couldn't get you out of my mind," she whispered, then suddenly looked away as if she'd said too much.

He knew then, with blinding instinctual clarity, that even if he couldn't have her forever, she wanted him to take what little time they had together and put it to good use.

Before he could move, she jumped the gun.

"Ah, hell," she said, rising unsteadily to her feet in the truck bed. "Here you are baby-sitting me when you could have your pick of any woman in Blue Spruce." She ran her fingers through her hair, then narrowed her eyes as she looked down at him. "Why didn't you ever get married?"

In answer, he grabbed hold of her ankle.

She almost fell over, then her eyes widened in surprise.

"No way."

"Yes."

She simply stared at him, almost refusing to believe.

"Yes," he whispered.

He said it with a quiet finality, with the sudden realization that before the night was over he would know this woman intimately, in all the ways he'd dreamed of during those long, lonely winters on his ranch.

He waited for her to respond, to answer him, her ankle still firmly grasped in his hand. He loosened his hold and slowly ran his fingers up her calf, then down to her ankle again. Caressing Meg was like touching one of his Arabians. The art of it was to guide them, bend them to your will without breaking their spirit. And she had such spirit; it was so much a part of this woman he'd loved for such a long time. It was why he'd never asked her to wait for him, to stay in Blue Spruce.

He'd wanted her to run free.

He waited now. Wondered what she would do. Knew from the look in her eyes that she wanted this to happen as much as he did. But he had to have her consent; she had to meet him halfway.

She didn't disappoint him.

His mouth went completely dry when she swiftly reached for the bottom of her black-ribbed tank top and slipped it over her head. Her bare breasts were full and perfectly shaped. He ached to touch her, to feel that warm, quivering flesh come alive beneath his fingers.

"Let's go skinny-dipping, Cowboy."

"My pleasure, Blue."

He shucked off his boots and stood beside her. She'd already unfastened her jeans and was starting to slide the zipper down when he stayed her restless fingers with a large hand.

"Let me."

Undressing her was like opening a small, exquisite gift. As he knelt and slid her jeans down her hips, he kissed the soft skin of her belly. She kicked the discarded clothing aside, then he hooked his fingers on the elastic of her sheer lace panties and pulled them down those perfectly shaped legs.

He couldn't speak, he was so overwhelmed with what was happening. This was so much better than any wistful, erotic dream he could have had. This was Meg, warm and willing and letting him know she'd thought about him the way he'd wondered about her.

He fought the urge to simply drag her down on the truck bed, cover her with his body and take her quickly, roughly, completely. He wanted to claim her, to make her his own, but he held off. For her sake, he wanted her to be comfortable with him, to respond to his lovemaking, to take both pleasure and joy from what he was about to do to her.

He sensed she didn't have as much experience as he had.

"No skinny-dipping," he whispered as he lowered her naked body onto the truck bed. The large sleeping bags had been unzipped, and now he placed her on one, then covered her naked body with the other. Then he divested himself of his shirt, jeans and briefs in record time.

He joined her beneath the sleeping bag, took her in

his arms, molded her against his body. She felt perfect, soft and smooth, smelling of some kind of flower and that wonderful warm scent that was hers alone. He kissed the nape of her neck, her collarbone, her cheek, her brow, and then brought his mouth down over hers.

Perfect. Sweet and hot and wild. Willing. Submissive in his hands, with that touch of fire and spirit he wanted to conquer then set free to take again and again. He couldn't think, he was so overwhelmed with sensation. When he'd first seen her walk into Duffy's Bar, he'd had no idea that within hours she would be naked in his arms, allowing him to do anything to her. Anything at all.

"Daniel," she whispered, her arms coming up around his neck. "Daniel." His name left her lips on a sigh; her full breasts felt hot as they pressed against his chest.

He couldn't seem to go slowly. Urgently, hot with desire, he moved down her body, taking one perfect breast into his palm, then the nipple into his mouth. Pulling on the tightly budded flesh, wrenching the sweetest-sounding moan from deep inside her. She twisted in his arms but he held her still, tasting, wanting, desiring.

He was a totally instinctual man, and he'd known it would be like this for them; none of the awkwardness of a first time, but that feeling of coming home to each other after a long, dry absence.

He pleasured her other breast, taking his time, kissing her belly, moving lower, breathing in her scent, parting her thighs. She stiffened slightly, as if unsure, and he moved back up, took her in his arms, kissed her.

Again and again and again, building that insistent masculine aggression until he felt the small, subtle feminine surrender, the boneless melting that told him she would give him whatever he wanted.

This time, when he moved lower, she didn't fight him. This time she let him spread her thighs and settle between them, tasting that dark, sweet part of her that promised him such incredible pleasure. She cried out as he pushed inside her, fingers and tongue insistent, demanding she take her pleasure.

He felt her excitement building, heard the sharp cries, pushed just that little bit harder until she reached it, felt the delicate contractions around his two fingers.

And he didn't even let it subside. As she came sliding down from that beautifully erotic ascent, he moved up her body, kissing her while his fingers continued to rub, stroke, lightly pinch and squeeze. She moaned against his mouth, then bit his lip, hard, when he made her come again, so soon, too soon, relentless in his conquest of her.

He held on to his control by sheer willpower. He loved her, didn't want to frighten her with the depth of his need. Daniel forced himself to stop, to give her time to accept what had happened and what still had to happen.

He let her rest then, while he stroked her back, long, smooth strokes from the nape of her neck to her buttocks. He cupped them, smoothed the skin, wanted to memorize every inch, every sound, each smell and caress. She wouldn't remain in Blue Spruce, but he would give her as much pleasure, as much of his love as he could while she let him.

He almost thought she'd fallen asleep until her fingers began to slowly, tentatively, explore his chest. She walked them through the sprinkling of chest hair, rubbed his flat nipples. He smiled down at her, could see the intent expression on her face. His breath caught when her hand moved slowly, seductively, down his abdomen.

She wanted to touch him; to know him, to know that part of him before she allowed him full access to her body. And he knew if she asked him to stop, he would, even though he was aroused to the point of physical pain. Although he badly needed release, he knew she could stop him with a look, the smallest sound, the tiniest of doubts.

But she didn't ask him to stop. His heart almost came out of his rib cage when he felt her close those delicate fingers around the swollen shaft of his erection.

"Oh."

He smiled at her breathy exclamation as she slowly measured the length and width of him, the aroused fullness. And although it was driving him out of his mind, he let her feel him, and come to accept that he wanted her to take him into her body; that he needed her, wanted her that way.

He'd had his share of women, none of whom he'd loved. Some he'd cared for, all of whom he'd treated well. He'd never promised them anything. But not one of them had come close to Meg.

He didn't want to hurt her. She'd felt incredibly tight when he'd touched her intimately, and even though he was an earthy man, a rancher who worked with animals and bred them, even though he knew the intricacies of the sexual act in all of its phases, he knew she needed time.

She stroked him, softly. He smoothed his hand over her inner thigh, felt the silky skin tremble beneath his touch, felt her legs gently part in surrender once again. He eased his hand against the hot wetness that threatened to make him lose his sanity and slowly, seductively rubbed.

She moaned again, her grip on him lessening.

He smiled; slipped a finger inside that delicate, feminine passage. She gripped him tightly, and he wondered how to make this work without causing her discomfort. It was obvious she hadn't been with a man in some time, and he didn't want to make this particular evening more difficult for her than it had to be.

"Meg," he whispered, kissing her.

"Mmm?"

"You can stop me at any time."

"That's so unfair," she whispered back.

"It's the way it is. Okay?"

She hesitated.

"I don't want you to be scared."

"I'm...not."

He waited. She'd never been able to lie to him before.

"A little," she breathed into his ear. He sensed she was too embarrassed to let him see her face. Her body was so alive, so responsive, so eager beneath his touch. Yet he sensed a part of her was afraid. And he felt big and clumsy and overwhelmed by the responsibility for her pleasure.

It was just so different with her.

"Lie on your side," he said, his voice gentle, calming her. She did, and with such trust as she looked up at him, it brought a sharp lump to his throat. He slid down next to her, facing her, stroked his hand over her buttock, cupped it, then moved his hand slowly up her leg. He raised it gently over his hip, positioning her for their mutual pleasure. Opening her to his touch.

He found the heart of her, hotly wet, and caressed that most sensitive bud softly with the tip of one finger, then slowly outlined that sweet, sweet passage.

She shuddered and closed her eyes. Groaned softly.

He reached down and carefully guided himself against her, then grazed the tip of his erection against her wet arousal, thoroughly preparing himself to ensure that their sensual joining would be easier for her. Then he began to slowly push inside.

At this angle, he knew he couldn't push as deeply and urgently as he wanted to. The way he was feeling about her, it would help him retain his self-control. He felt her open around him, felt delicate muscles relax and barely let him in, then grasp him tightly. This was sensual agony.

He heard the quick, soft intake of her breath as those same muscles closed around the head of his arousal.

"Oh," she breathed, but she didn't sound as if she were in pain. He bit his lip, concentrating on pleasuring her, then pushed farther. Slowly. Gently. She moaned, but he didn't sense she was in pain. Quite the contrary. Now that he was sheathed inside her, he grasped her hips, held her firmly, made her take him deeper. Using exquisite control, he began to stroke her, gently at first, paying close attention to the sounds she made, the movement of her hips.

She tilted her hips, silently yearning, asking him to come even closer. He complied, then came up against the natural limitations the position imposed. He'd assumed he would find his release this way, for he didn't want to force his pleasure at her expense. But she surprised him again.

She came, crying out. In the aftermath of her climax, she grasped his shoulders, her nails biting into his skin. She pulled, causing him to roll over her, up on top of her and slide all the way in.

Heaven. Absolute, exquisite heaven. She clutched him tighter than a fist, and felt so very hot. He pulled back, then pushed forward, all the way inside. Again. Again. Relentlessly continuing the erotic night rhythm. And she began those moans, deep in the back of her throat. He smiled against her hair, then suddenly he couldn't smile, couldn't stop; pumped harder and harder as he became caught up in the urgent and deeply instinctual needs of his sexual release.

Afterward he rolled off her, almost ashamed of how quickly he'd come. He'd wanted to last, make it last forever with her; but it had been too much. He'd felt as if he'd been waiting for years for her, that this was the culmination of everything he'd ever felt for her.

She snuggled up against him in the circle of his arms. He couldn't have spoken or moved if his life had depended on it, so he simply kissed her neck, breathed in the soft scent of her hair, wrapped his arm heavily around her waist, and slept.

HER EYES OPENED almost forty-five minutes later, and she stretched, winced, then smiled. Those shots of tequila hadn't even given her a headache. And she was suddenly glad that Daniel had been gentleman enough to drink with her, because she wasn't at all sure they would have made love like they had if they'd both been sober.

But now there was no turning back.

She eased away from him, then studied his face as he slept. He looked so relaxed, and she had the feeling it was as much from sexual release as from sleep. There had been so much intensity in his lovemaking—as if he'd been boiling with emotion inside. She'd loved being the recipient.

Meg watched him as she remembered each detail. She felt no shame, and absolutely no regrets. She'd known Daniel for years, secretly yearned after him the entire time; what had just happened in the back of his truck seemed so right.

She snuggled up against him and came into contact with a very impressive erection.

Feeling mischievous, she kissed him on the tip of his nose and watched as he slowly woke up.

"Sleepy," she whispered. "And sexy." Her hand drifted lower, caught him, held him.

That woke him up fast. He smiled, those dark gray eyes lighting with a passion, an intensity that he had to have kept in check before. She'd never seen him look like that before. At her, or at anyone.

He kissed her. Lazily. Thoroughly. Then his lips brushed her ear as he whispered, "Don't play unless you want to pay."

She laughed, delighted, and kept a firm hold.

"You're asking for it, Blue."

"I don't know how I can be much more obvious."

"It'll be a long, slow ride this time," he said, with unconscious male arrogance. She shivered in restless anticipation. Meg couldn't think of anything she would like more. He misinterpreted the gesture and tucked the insulated sleeping bag high around her shoulders. Even during the summer, Colorado nights could be cool. "Cold?"

"Not with you."

"Do you want to go back to the ranch?"

She thought of that long, slow, sexy ride he promised her, with her back pressed against the slightly padded, hard metal truck bed. She thought of making him lie back and letting her get on top of him, the sleeping bag slipping down over her shoulders, her nipples peaking in response to the cool night air.

Then she thought of his ranch. The two of them all alone. A warm, soft, large bed. Complete privacy for whatever he had in mind for her. And most important, the hot bath she was going to need desperately when this long, pleasurable night was over.

As always, Daniel was putting her needs first.

"I'd like to go back to your ranch."

He surprised her then, jumping out of the truck bed and starting the vehicle. Then he came back, wrapped her snugly in one of the sleeping bags and settled her in the passenger seat. He'd turned on the heater and she luxuriated in the blast of warm air. Her muscles had cramped slightly as she'd dozed outside in the night.

She watched him in the side mirror as he shrugged into his clothing, gathered hers, then climbed into the driver's seat and put the truck in Reverse. They backed away from the lakefront, then he turned and headed toward the two-lane highway.

She reached for his hand from beneath the warm sleeping bag, caught it, and rested their joined fingers against his denim-clad thigh.

"You know, we never did get to skinny-dip," she said wistfully. The thought of swimming completely naked with Daniel gave her great pleasure.

"We will," he said, his eyes on the road as he turned onto the highway.

"Promise?"

He gave her a quick look and her stomach clenched in involuntary delight at the proprietary look in those dark gray eyes.

"Count on it."

3

THE WILLETT RANCH house looked totally different in the moonlight. It took Meg a couple of seconds to realize it *was* a totally different house.

"Daniel?" She didn't quite know what to say. The same property, the same view of the mountains, the corrals, but the *house*...

"I tore down the old farmhouse four years ago," he said quietly. He'd parked the truck by one of the corrals, and now they sat, silent, as Meg watched the moonlight play over the rooftop of the one-story ranch house. The sky, cloudless and dark, set off the moon to perfection.

She liked this new house. She could barely remember the two-story Victorian farmhouse that had been there before. Intuitively, she wondered if Daniel had decided to raze the original structure to the ground in order to silence some of the more unpleasant memories.

Meg didn't want to ask, didn't want to make him remember the painful times, didn't want to ruin the mood. She'd been delighted at the way he'd laughed at her struggles to get dressed inside the truck as they'd sped along the deserted highway.

"We're like a couple of teenagers," she'd muttered,

then couldn't help breaking up as he'd continued laughing.

Now, staring at the house, she wondered. There were so many questions she wanted to ask him, but she sensed now was not the time.

"Would you like to see it?" he asked.

She knew what he was really asking her. If she wanted, he would turn around and take her straight home, to the relative safety of her motel room in town. Or she could make the decision to spend the night with him.

She knew what she wanted.

"Yes."

Meg followed Daniel toward the front door, her boots crunching on the gravel drive. As they approached the house, shadowy canine forms ran up to them, tongues lolling, tails swishing, eager whines asking for affection.

"Hunter?" she asked as she knelt to pet the small, shepherd mix. Even in the bright moonlight, she could see kindness in the dog's expression.

Daniel nodded his head.

Two other dogs joined them, both mutts, both small, one with a definite limp. Meg shot a questioning glance at Daniel, and he said, "I found them out by the highway at different times. Digger had some barbed wire twined around his neck, and I guess Molly had been thrown out of a car. Her leg was broken, and I could never get it to heal right."

Then she remembered. Daniel had wanted to be a vet. He'd always had a way with animals, and did a lot of his own work, as most ranchers did. He had a quiet presence that seemed to soothe animals. They trusted him.

Meg noticed that the smaller of the two mutts, the black-and-white Molly, gave her a wide berth. She didn't quite trust Meg, but the look the dog turned on Daniel was adoring. A swift lump came to her throat, at the thought of Daniel spotting the little dog, carrying her inside, setting the leg as best he could before taking her to the vet; then watching over her, nursing her, until the small dog could get up and around by herself.

"She's beautiful," Meg said, indicating Molly.

"She'll come around in a bit," he said as he strode up the steps to the small front porch and unlocked the door. "Once she figures out she doesn't have to be afraid of you."

She had a curious sense of anticipation as she followed Daniel inside. The last time she'd been out to the Willett ranch had been shortly before her graduation. She remembered the large Victorian as being filled with confusion, the wraparound porch crowded with chairs, benches, tables and *stuff*. The kitchen cupboards had been crammed, the large table in the dining room dusty.

The confusion inside the farmhouse had been a direct reflection of what was inside Erna Willett's mind. Daniel's mother had grown increasingly unstable, living in her own world and only facing reality in small, measured amounts. Only the barn and the henhouse, the corrals and stables had been pristine and clean.

Now, walking inside, she realized she was about to see the home Daniel had created for himself. A flood of emotion threatened to overwhelm her, and she suddenly realized she was glad he'd never married. Coming here to meet a Mrs. Daniel Willett would have been too hard.

Her first impression was one of peace. The second, of warmth—so different from her mother's spacious-but-cold apartment in Manhattan. The third, that he'd created a genuine home, and she was glad for him.

The entranceway opened into a large living room, with the kitchen directly to the right. It was tucked in the corner, but didn't give the impression of being small. A long counter served as the table, and she noticed a large chocolate bundt cake on a plate, the chocolate icing shiny in the soft light.

Daniel baking? It didn't make sense. Even Erna hadn't had time for what she called "fancy cooking." It had been meat and potatoes all the way with the Willetts she'd known.

He caught the direction of her gaze. "Betty Sue down the road. Once in a while she drops something by. In exchange for eggs."

Men could be so dense. Meg thought Betty Sue was probably coming by for a lot more than eggs, but she didn't say anything.

Still looking around, she walked past the kitchen and into the large sitting room. A huge stone fireplace dominated one wall, with built-in bookshelves on either side. Two couches faced each other, along with several extremely comfortable-looking chairs. An afghan in muted earth tones was draped across the back of one of the couches, a wool blanket with a vivid Native American design across the other.

In front of the fire, over the regular carpeting, was a

large, well-worn rag rug that obviously belonged to the dogs, as they all three hunkered down on it and stretched out with appreciative sighs and grunts.

She smiled.

Meg could sense his eyes on her as she walked the length of the room, then studied the books on the shelves. Lots of nonfiction that concerned agriculture, farming and animal husbandry, but fiction as well. Some of her favorite authors.

She stopped when she caught sight of a copy of her novel.

"I'd like you to sign it for me," he said. Daniel silently came up behind her and placed two careful hands on her shoulders. She put one of her hands on top of his, and absently stroked the warm fingers.

"I will. But I have to think for a little bit."

"Fair enough." He stepped back, breaking contact, and she sensed he was going to let her explore some more.

One door obviously led down to some sort of basement or even a garage. Another led into the front room, a formal living room. This one had comfortable, masculine-looking furniture in it as well, and another fireplace. She could picture Daniel sitting here with his dogs, on a cold winter night. They would all be snug and cozy after going out to the barn to feed his horses.

She glanced back at him, standing by the large stone fireplace. "Can I snoop through the rest?"

He nodded. "I'll make us some coffee."

She walked down the hallway, glancing inside two bedrooms. Guest rooms. Simple and serene. Blues, greens and browns. The colors you would find in nature. And then what had to be a den, with Daniel's desk and books. A computer. Obviously it was where he conducted business and paid his bills.

The walls of this room were lined with framed photos of his brothers. Joe, with his wife and two little girls. Brett, his hair windblown, grinning and standing by a plane. Alec with a girl she didn't recognize, but from the look in his eyes she guessed it was the fiancée from Atlanta.

The Arabians. A stiff, formal shot of Erna. Several photos of Bob Willett, Daniel's father. He'd been a strong man, whose life had ended when a drunk driver had plowed into his truck one night on his way home from town, leaving Erna to cope with four boisterous young boys and a ranch she'd apparently never wanted in the first place.

A shot of Molly, her expression indignant, her fluffy hair covered with water and soapsuds. A profile of Hunter, a close-up of Digger.

A picture of her.

On the corral fence, with Alec. She had to be all of sixteen years old, her long hair pulled back off her face in a single braid down her back, a red bandana twisted into a headband. Both of them had flecks of white paint on their faces, and Alec was trying to swipe at her with a wet paintbrush as she fended him off.

Instantly she thought back to the summer day she'd helped paint one of the corral fences. And remembered that Brett, mischief maker that he was, had brought out the camera and caught the moment.

Alec hadn't saved the photo. Daniel had.

She backed away from it, walked out of his office as

if she'd been caught looking at something too private, continued down the hall and stepped into his bedroom.

It felt like him. The bed frame was warm, golden oak, the quilt hand-pieced in dark reds, blues and grays. For a moment she wondered if Betty Sue had been coming by to give more than chocolate cake.

He was a neat, spare man. Nothing was out of place, yet the room looked warm and inviting—not the resting place of a man who was obsessively clean or compulsive about it. One of the windows looked out toward the barn, and she knew that in the morning this room would be flooded with eastern sunlight. Then she realized all the windows in this new house were large, not small and dusty—and closed—as they'd been in the old Victorian.

Meg's attention went back to the bed, and she thought of sharing it with Daniel tonight. She glanced at the clock—eleven twenty-three. They'd left Duffy's rather soon after the reunion had begun at seven that evening, so despite the time spent out at the lake, it still wasn't after midnight.

The bed looked comforting and inviting. Without even knowing where the thought came from, Meg realized she wished she never had to leave.

Calm down. You're reacting this way because you have some tough decisions to make, and it would be just fine with you to hide out here with Daniel, play the live-in girlfriend and never have to make a decision again in your life—

With that thought, she turned and walked swiftly out of the bedroom, back toward the kitchen and Daniel and coffee.

THE CHOCOLATE CAKE was incredibly good.

"Do you think she'd give me the recipe?" Meg asked as she squashed together the last few moist crumbs on her plate with her fork. She was even considering going for a second piece. A small one, of course.

"You bake?"

The surprised look on Daniel's face was priceless, and Meg started to laugh, her mouth still full of chocolate.

"I have been known to cook a few things in this lifetime."

"I didn't mean it that way." Now Daniel looked uncomfortable.

"I know. No offense taken. This is really good."

"I'll let her know."

"Daniel, somehow I don't think Betty Sue is going to like hearing about how another woman enjoyed her cake in your house late one night, if you get my drift."

He started to laugh so hard that he almost spilled his coffee. "Meg, she's married to Donald Herlihy and they have four children. Two girls and twin boys."

"Oh." Now she felt incredibly small. Mean. Petty.

He smiled, and her heart turned over.

I'm jealous. I can't believe it, but I'm jealous of Betty Sue because she gets to live down the road from him and bake him chocolate cake.

She decided to try and save the situation.

"They must be incredible eggs," she said.

He merely laughed and cut her another slice of cake.

"WOULD YOU LIKE TO sleep in another bedroom?"

Meg stood in Daniel's bedroom, staring at the bed.

They'd finished their cake and coffee, and now this particular decision loomed in front of her.

"No."

"You're sure, Blue?"

"No."

He sighed. "At least you're honest."

She turned to face him. "I'm just... It happened so fast, and..."

"I know." He started toward the door. "I'll get the room next door ready."

"No, I... What I'd really like is... Could we..."

He waited—so patiently that it almost tore her heart out.

"I'd like to sleep with you—"

"But no sex." He finished the sentence for her. She looked up at him uncertainly.

"Would that be terrible? Would you think I was teasing you?"

"I'd think you just wanted to slow things down a little. But still be close."

"That's it."

"That's fine, Blue."

She sat on the edge of the large bed and watched while he rummaged through his dresser. He tossed her one of his undershirts.

"I'll get ready in the bathroom," she said.

When she came back out, he was already beneath the covers, and the only light in the room came from the small lamp on the bedside table.

His undershirt came to her mid-thigh, so she felt completely covered up. Daniel was a gentleman. If he gave her his word, she knew she could trust him.

"Okay." She gave him a bright smile and slid beneath the sheets, then plumped up her pillow and lay down on her back. She stared at the ceiling, not quite able to meet his eyes.

He turned off the light.

After a few moments of silence, she whispered, "I always thought about what it would be like."

"What?"

"Sleeping with you."

"Me, too."

"You did?"

"All the time, when I was a teenager." She could hear the smile in his voice.

"Boy, the years we wasted."

"I'll second that." She heard him sigh. "Blue, you can move a little closer. I won't bite, and I promise not to start anything."

"Hmm." She considered this. "What are you wearing?"

"Underwear and...my socks."

"Socks?" Daniel was an incredibly sexy man, and the thought of him in next to nothing but a pair of socks was funny.

"My feet sometimes get cold." He laughed when she didn't reply right away. "Though out in that truck I was warm to the tips of my toes."

"Hot, you mean." She snuggled closer. "A promise is a promise. I know you'll keep your word."

"On my honor."

It felt so good to melt against him—the warmth of his body, the rough texture of his chest hair, that place on his shoulder where her head fit perfectly.

"I'm glad it finally happened," she said softly, her eyelids growing heavy.

"I am too, honey," she thought she heard him whisper as she drifted off to sleep.

SHE WOKE UP A FEW hours later to the sound of his deep breathing. And wondered if she'd ever felt anything as comforting as sleeping in Daniel's arms.

They slept like spoons, her back to his front. His body seemed to radiate warmth, and she snuggled against him, burrowing closer, sighing with sheer feminine delight at the feel of his arms around her. She liked lying with her head on his arm, her feet twined around his muscular legs.

Meg rubbed his hair-roughened legs with her bare feet, then turned slightly so she was lying on her back while he remained deeply asleep, on his side. She inched back just enough so she could study Daniel's face.

Years ago, the hardest thing in the world had been leaving him, driving her Jeep out of Blue Spruce and getting on the interstate to Los Angeles. If it hadn't been for her mother, and all the opinions she'd been force-fed over the years, she might have been content to be a rancher's wife.

Meg closed her eyes. She wasn't being entirely honest with herself. Even with her mother's standards and opinions always lying in wait at the back of her mind, she'd wanted to see the world. And she had. And now, back in Blue Spruce, in Daniel's house and in his arms, there was no place on earth that felt more right.

What were you running from?

He sighed, his arm tightening as he pulled her closer. Meg relaxed, let her body slide against his. And registered the fact that unconsciously, in sleep, he wanted her. That, or he was having an extremely enjoyable dream.

She moved closer. Kissed his neck. Breathed in the scent of him; that clean, masculine warmth. Kissed him again, and grinned at the slightly dazed expression on his face as he started to surface.

"Meg?" he said softly. But he kissed her back.

"Forget what I said," she whispered against his mouth.

"Meg, I—"

"I changed my mind. Forget that promise."

She reached for him.

He groaned.

She smiled against his mouth as she kissed him.

He slid his tongue inside her mouth and she was lost.

Her last semiconscious thought as he moved over her and settled his body between her thighs was that she was going to get that long, slow ride after all.

HE WOKE UP, AS MOST ranchers do, just before sunrise.

Pale light had just touched the horizon as Daniel opened his eyes. The first thing he sensed was how right it felt to hold Meg in his arms. The second thought that entered his head was that if he wasn't careful, he wouldn't be able to let her go. He would make a fool of himself and lose her once again.

Be content that you'll have this time with her. It's more than you believed you would ever have.

He watched her. The gentle rise and fall of her chest. The way the light began to play with her bright blond hair. The sooty smudge of her eyelashes against her cheeks, the little bit of makeup that had come off from last night. She'd pulled the undershirt on and climbed straight into bed with him, not even bothering to wash her face. So like Meg, to jump right in. He loved her boldness, the passionate way she'd always faced life and everything it had to offer.

Now he realized it was a peculiar form of torment— to have her this close and yet not at all. In her own way, she was like Molly, circling and circling, watching with wary eyes, making sure. He didn't know anything about her life in Los Angeles; if any man had broken her heart, treated her badly. He knew she'd left Blue Spruce wanting to run, to test her limits, to fly high and free.

And she had.

Daniel studied her as the bedroom slowly lightened. He'd never considered himself as having a type, a particular sort of woman he preferred, but now he had to admit Meg was it. Over the years, he'd subconsciously compared every woman he'd taken out to her. This petite blonde, so filled with fire and laughter, with zany ideas, had captured his heart when he was still a boy. No one else had ever even come close.

She had seemed exotic and exciting. Different from the other people around Blue Spruce. Probably partly because of the way her mother had blown into town and bought the largest house on Main Street. The way she'd swept into the local stores and demanded various services. No one had ever seen anyone like Antonia Prescott.

Fresh from Manhattan, hurting from a divorce, determined to start over again, the woman had dragged her young daughter west and settled in the small town at the foot of the Rockies. Meg had been entering high school that year. A freshman.

Daniel smiled, remembering. He'd been walking out onto the football field to give his brother Alec a message before he left for home when he'd first seen Meg. Hal Evert, the town bully, had been mashing Pete Cunningham's face into the dirt. The short, small freshman hadn't been a match for the muscle-bound senior. And this confrontation was taking place in a corner of the playing field, where not too many people would notice what went on.

He'd changed course, deciding instantaneously to confront Hal, when an energetic blur of a figure had leaped on top of Hal's back and started pummeling him.

"Back off, you big oaf!"

He'd heard the angry words float over the playing field and been astonished when he suddenly realized that the angry voice was *feminine.* Then he'd seen the long braid down her back, and the jeans-clad figure had quickly become someone else who needed protection.

Hal had stopped pounding on Pete, but now looked like an angry gorilla with an especially pesky mosquito on its back. He whirled and whirled, arms flailing, trying to simply force Meg off, but she continued to pummel him, with more passion and anger than actual

fighting skill. By the time Daniel had reached the two
of them and pulled Meg off Hal, she'd managed to get
in a few good licks of her own.

He'd pushed her behind him when Hal started toward her.

"This isn't your fight," the muscle-bound senior had
said angrily, wiping a thin line of blood from the corner of his lip.

"You shouldn't be hitting a boy half your size. Or a
girl." Daniel's heart had been pounding triple time, but
he hadn't backed down. His daddy had always taught
him to stand firm, to help anyone in trouble. This was
simply one of those times, and he knew what he had to
do.

"Get out of my way," Hal had snarled, hatred in his
eyes, and clearly mortified that a girl, and a small one
at that, had gotten the upper hand. "I'm gonna teach
this little girl a lesson she won't soon forget."

"No."

They'd fought, rolling in the dirt like a couple of
dogs. Coach Riley had seen them, and within the half
hour, Hal, Pete, Daniel and Meg had all found themselves in Principal Hodgman's office. The coach had
told the principal what he'd seen, and now the flustered man had to do what he thought was best.

"I'm calling all your parents," he'd said quietly. A
mild-looking man with gray receding hair and
perpetually startled eyes behind his spectacles, Principal Hodgman had the manner of a man who didn't
quite know how he'd ended up in the principal's chair.

Hal had simply sat back, his manner arrogant, his
legs spread. Even Daniel, despite how little time he

spent in town, knew Hal's father wouldn't be at work. He would be at The End, a bar located at the edge of town. Principal Hodgman wouldn't be able to contact the man. And if he did, Hal's father wouldn't really care.

Pete's father had come first, a nervous, flustered sort of man. He'd fussed over his son, glared at Meg, Daniel and Hal, then escorted his subdued offspring home for the day.

Bob Willett had arrived next. Daniel's eyes still stung whenever he remembered his father, and this time was no exception. He wiped at his eyes as he remembered his father, in worn jeans, scuffed work boots, a wool plaid shirt and sheepskin jacket, coming into the principal's office on that crisp fall afternoon.

"Mr. Willett, your son—" Principal Hodgman had begun, almost as if he had to get his side of the story in as quickly as possible.

"I'd like to talk to Daniel, if I might," Bob had said, and Daniel had seen the quiet strength that was so much a part of his father. His heart had been glad.

He'd told his father exactly what had happened, and halfway through the tale, his daddy's warm hand had come to rest on his shoulder, telling him without words that they were in this problem together, that they were family, that there was nothing the two of them couldn't solve.

"Well," Bob Willett had said, turning toward the principal. "We've got a misunderstanding here, because my boy acted exactly the way I would have expected him to. Hal was beating on a younger boy, and then threatened a girl. Daniel saw what he had to do, and did it."

"But Mr. Willett, we don't allow fighting on school grounds."

"I understand, and I agree it's a good rule. But what would you have had Daniel do? Walk on by?"

The principal was clearly stumped by this one.

"He told Hal he didn't want a fight, but he couldn't have left this young lady and that other boy without protection. Don't you understand the situation he was in?"

While the principal thought about this, Antonia Prescott had entered the office, and Daniel had gotten his first look at Meg's mother. His instinctual impressions had been swift. Beautiful, but cold. Expensively dressed and made-up, diamond earrings flashing, auburn hair swept up on top of her head in an elegant twist.

But her green eyes had been glacial.

"Meg." Absolute disapproval had etched the older woman's expression. Daniel had watched as Meg had glanced quickly up at her mother, then down at the tile floor, ashamed.

"Oh, Meg. Fighting is not proper behavior for people like us."

He'd watched as the girl's cheeks had heated with painfully embarrassed color.

"Do you have anything to say for yourself?"

"No, Mother."

He'd hurt for her then. The two words had been forced out of her mouth. Barely whispered.

Antonia had glanced at the principal in a regal manner, as though she felt she'd been disturbed by something inconsequential.

"Do what you have to." She'd shaken her head. "There are times when I just don't know what to do with her." Then she'd swept out of the office, an incredibly lush fur coat around her shoulders, expensive scent trailing in her wake.

Meg had continued to look down at the floor.

"Well." Principal Hodgman had cleared his throat. "Well. I'm going to have to give you all detention after school. For two weeks."

"I need Daniel at home," Bob Willett had said quietly.

"Then what would you have me do?" the principal had asked in exasperation.

Daniel had watched as his father thought, and had wondered what he was about to suggest.

"Let the young boy be. Pete's already been frightened enough. He had no part in the fighting."

"Fair enough." Principal Hodgman had nodded his head.

"Why don't you let me come pick up Daniel, Meg and Hal after school each day for a week or so, and let them work off some of their energy?"

The principal hesitated.

"I don't know how sitting in a room for an hour staring out the window is going to teach them anything." Daniel had been so proud of his father as he'd leaned across the principal's desk, his palms flat on the smooth, wooden surface. "I'll keep them busy, and get them thinking."

"All right." The principal had actually seemed relieved that someone else was taking on the burden of the final decision.

So that was what his father had done. Every day at three he'd been out front, parked in the circular drive of the high school in his battered old pickup truck. He'd driven them out to the ranch and given them chores to do. And while Hal and Meg had done theirs, he'd talked to them.

"They're hurting," he'd told Daniel one night as they'd washed up for dinner. "Each in their different ways, but they're hurting. That's what the fighting was about."

Working at the ranch had created a healing time for Hal, an angry youth who didn't know where he was going or how to create his own future. After he'd graduated from high school, Bob Willett had helped him find a place on a neighboring ranch two hours away from Blue Spruce. It was important to Hal that no one knew about his drunk of a father or where he'd come from. He wanted a fresh start. A new life. He didn't want to be judged anymore.

Daniel remembered that Hal had come back to Blue Spruce for Bob Willett's funeral, but not for his own father's.

And Meg. She'd simply charmed his whole family. Especially Alec. There had always been a little more laughter in the Willett family when she was around.

But she'd had a serious side as well, and had spent several evenings talking with his father. About what, Daniel wasn't sure, but he knew those talks had probably had something to do with her mother. He'd walked in on her crying in the barn one time, leaning on his daddy's shoulder. And he'd been glad he could share his father with her.

She'd been at the funeral, too. Her mother had chosen not to attend, but Meg had walked twelve blocks through a severe snowstorm to get to Nevin's Funeral Parlor. She'd looked as devastated as any of the Willetts had felt as she'd stared at that closed casket.

Daniel slipped back into the present as he felt a wet, canine nose nudge his bare shoulder. Glancing behind him, he saw Hunter's wise, compassionate eyes. She was looking at him as if asking, "Aren't we going out and starting our chores this morning?"

He eased out of bed, careful not to disturb Meg. He knew what it had cost her, coming back to Blue Spruce. Her mother had made it almost impossible for Meg to simply fit in. But she'd somehow managed, on the sheer strength of her sunny personality.

Now, knowing she had a dinner dance at the country club this evening, and a chicken barbecue to get through Sunday afternoon, Daniel decided to let her sleep in. He would do his chores, then clean up and check in on her. And when she got up, he would make her breakfast.

But beyond the next forty-eight hours, he didn't have a clue what would happen. The woman he'd fallen in love with when he'd turned sixteen finally lay sleeping in his bed, in his home. She'd always had his heart. Now, at thirty, he had no idea how he was going to ask her to stay.

Or if he even had the right to.

4

MEG SLEPT LIKE THE DEAD until the muted ring of the bedside phone woke her. Groggily she awakened, glancing around the strange, light-filled bedroom and taking several seconds to recognize where she was.

She didn't do mornings well.

On the fourth ring, she picked up. She hadn't noticed an answering machine in Daniel's home. He was probably out in the barn, and she was certainly capable of taking a message.

"H'lo?" She pushed a hand through her hair, then stifled a yawn.

"Don't kill us," a familiar voice whispered.

Heather.

"Meg, we went to your motel afterward, and waited around for hours," Laura chimed in on another extension. "We thought you might have gone out with Daniel somewhere, but we had no idea—"

Sleeping with Daniel was something so private, so deeply intimate. Meg realized she didn't want to share this particular part of her life with anyone. Yet.

"I fell asleep on his living-room couch." She yawned again, for extra good measure. "He must have carried me into one of the guest bedrooms."

"Oh." Heather sounded disappointed. "I don't think

I could have spent the night with Daniel Willett and not at least tried something."

"Hmm." Meg waited, knowing her two friends had to have something in mind.

"Are you...are you still going to the dinner dance tonight?" Laura asked.

Comprehension dawned. They were both afraid that what they'd done had soured the whole reunion for her.

"Of course I am. I'm even looking forward to it." She sat up in bed, determined to be totally honest about this entire misunderstanding. Antonia Prescott, she wasn't. If there was one thing Meg didn't want to emulate, it was her mother's airs and half-truths; the way she'd always tried to appear better than anyone else.

"You are?" Now Heather sounded worried.

"I am." Meg took a deep breath. "Both of you realize I'll have to come clean."

"Oh, no, Meg—"

"You can't—"

"Yes, I can, and I have to. For my own peace of mind." Meg glanced at the bedroom window as she caught a flash of movement out of the corner of her eye. Daniel was striding toward the house, the three dogs at his heels, running and jumping with abandon.

"Look, I've got to go. I'm having breakfast with Daniel and I should be back in town in about an hour and a half. Let me call you— No, let me meet you guys at Laura's house when I get back. Okay?"

Dead silence.

"Okay?"

"Yeah," Laura said finally. Meg could tell they

weren't happy at the idea of her telling the townspeople of Blue Spruce the truth.

"Okay. Gotta go." And with that, Meg hung up the phone, slid out from beneath the covers of Daniel's big warm bed, and darted into the bathroom.

DANIEL HEARD THE SHOWER running before he reached his bedroom door and stopped. Even though he'd grown up in a house with three brothers, he still knew that Meg would want her privacy.

So he snapped his fingers, rounded up the overeager dogs, and headed toward the kitchen to prepare the large batch of pancakes he planned to serve for breakfast.

THE SHOWER FELT heavenly.

Meg simply stood beneath the hot, steaming water and let it sluice down her body. Even though she and Daniel weren't exactly in the running for the sexual Olympics, and last night's lovemaking had been gentle and tender—though passionate—she still found herself aching in a number of interesting places.

She paused as she lathered shampoo into her hair. The right word was *thorough*. He'd been thorough with her; there wasn't a place on her body he hadn't explored. It had been as if they'd both been making up for that long, long wait. They'd finally caught up, and their fantasies had become reality.

With a vengeance. She smiled, then ducked her head beneath the strong, hot spray, enjoying the sensation of all that mousse being rinsed away. At home, when working, she barely did anything with her hair. It was only here, just before walking into Duffy's Tavern and having to face all her classmates again, that she'd felt she had to...be something she wasn't. But only because her career was so precarious at the moment.

Everyone did that at times, didn't they?

She grabbed a bar of soap and began to lather her body. It didn't even feel like her own. She felt more alive, as if her skin were more sensitive. As if her entire body were humming. So alive.

So *happy*.

She'd wanted to make love to Daniel for such a long time, and the reality of being in his bed, in his arms, and taking his body inside hers had far exceeded any sexual fantasy she could have created.

She'd left Blue Spruce a virgin, because the only man she'd wanted to sleep with was Daniel. And she'd lost her virginity late, to a television writer she dated for almost a year. She'd met him at a party in Santa Monica, taken one look at him, and decided the time had come.

But that whole experience couldn't hold a candle to being with Daniel.

She rinsed, turned off the water and stepped outside the shower stall and onto a thick blue bath mat. Reaching for a towel, she wrapped it around her body, then took another and started drying her hair.

The body held a wisdom she was slowly beginning to see she should have listened to. With Daniel, everything felt right. There hadn't been the awkwardness, the uncertainty of the usual first time. They'd both dived in like dolphins at play in the ocean. They'd both been so eager to get close.

Meg finished drying her hair, hung up the towel, then sat down on the edge of the tub.

What now?

She closed her eyes, taking a brief respite from all she had to face in the next forty-eight hours. All she really wanted to do was ask Daniel to drag her back to bed and not leave his secluded bedroom for a week.

The second time they'd made love had been better than the first, because in a strange sort of way, they'd both known what was coming. It hadn't had the urgency, the sense of discovery, of that first time. It had been long and slow and hot, without being rushed; with plenty of desire, both of them luxuriously cocooned in that big bed.

He'd made her feel so safe, yet so wild. So cherished. And desired. Deeply desired. He'd given over so much in that bed; he'd given over himself, and she'd responded in kind. In a strange way, Meg knew she had never really made love before last night.

Not with her heart, anyway.

She'd left her clothing in a neat, folded pile on top of the clothes hamper, and now she reached for that same clothing and dressed quickly. Finding a comb, she slicked it through her hair, then took a quick look at herself in the mirror.

No makeup. No masks. Naked skin, glowing skin. Skin that had that "Boy, did *I* have a great time last night" look to it. Her eyes sparkled, and her lips kept curving into a happy little smile.

She couldn't wait to see Daniel.

WHEN SHE CAME INTO the room, she quite literally took his breath away. And he knew at that moment that he'd always imagined her here at his ranch, in this room, sharing meals with him. Laughing. Talking. It hit him hard, deep in his chest, as he watched Meg take a seat at the breakfast bar and smile up at him.

"Hi," she said.

He wanted to express his feelings, but he wasn't a man at ease with words. It always took him a while to be able to articulate what it was he felt. Many times he simply couldn't. So instead, he smiled back at her infectious happiness and set a plate of pancakes in front of her, then butter, maple syrup and orange juice.

"Oh! Blueberries!" Her tone was reverent as she cut off a pat of butter and began spreading it around. And he was glad he'd taken the time to learn how to cook a few things well, cornmeal blueberry pancakes being one of them.

"These are great," she said, her mouth full, already intent on another bite. Daniel almost laughed as he slid another serving of pancakes onto a plate and joined her.

"You're a good cook," she said, and took a swallow of her juice.

Then he did laugh.

"Well, you *are*."

"I would've starved out here if I hadn't learned a few things." He buttered his pancakes, then poured on the syrup. "And I always did love pancakes."

"These are amazing—" He watched as she caught sight of Molly out of the corner of her eye.

"She likes them, too," Daniel said quietly.

"Can I give her a little?"

He nodded.

She tore off a corner of one pancake that wasn't too syrupy, then lowered her hand to dog level. And Daniel sensed Meg saw the conflict in Molly's tentative expression. But her hand remained steady, and in the end, the promise of pancakes proved too much for the fluffy little dog. Molly snuck up, then darted her muzzle out and snatched the piece of pancake out of Meg's outstretched hand.

"I'm impressed," Daniel said. "It took me a lot longer to have her eating out of my hand."

"You paved the way." Meg turned back to her meal, and Daniel realized yet another thing he enjoyed about her. She liked to eat, possessed a hearty appetite. He didn't know where she put it, because she couldn't weigh over a hundred pounds, even soaking wet. But he loved the way she simply dug into his pancakes with total enthusiasm.

She made love much the same way.

He didn't want to ask her if there was anyone waiting for her in Los Angeles. He knew it was none of his business. She'd told him there was no one last night, but he couldn't imagine a woman like Meg without at least one serious man in her life. If not several. If he found her this irresistible, what man wouldn't?

And he certainly didn't want to think that he might simply have been an itch she'd been wanting to scratch for a long time. To satisfy curiosity that had been building for quite a few years. To get something out of her system before she returned to the West Coast.

It hadn't felt that way. It had felt to him—as he'd entered her warm, willing body—as if he were coming home. To her. To the one place in the world he'd always wanted to be. But he wasn't sure it had been the same for her, and he was honest enough to admit he was terrified of asking.

He could gentle a wild horse, give a shot to a calf. Muck out the messiest stall or face down an angry, frustrated bull during breeding season. Look at the sky, feel the pressure of the wind, the electricity in the air, and be able to tell if a storm was approaching. These things his father had taught him, and more. But growing up with his younger brothers, under his mother's harsh eye, he felt sorely lacking in the knowledge of how to deal with what he was feeling.

More than anything, he didn't want to spill his heart out to Meg, to reveal his deepest feelings and see that she didn't return them. He'd worked hard all his life; he didn't know any other way. He just didn't have a whole lot of faith that what he had built here on this piece of land just outside Blue Spruce would be enough for her.

So he ate his pancakes, answered her questions, simply enjoyed looking at her. In many ways, she was so easy to be with. So loving and giving. So *alive*.

Everything that he felt he was not.

More than anything, he wanted her to know how he really felt about her. He'd tried to tell her—with his body—last night. But his chest constricted at the thought of actually saying the words. He finished most of his pancakes, scraped the rest of his plate into the bowl of the eagerly waiting Molly, then told Meg he would drive her back into town.

SHE WONDERED, all the way back to the motel, what she'd done to change the mood. Because somewhere along the way, she'd lost him.

It was as if Daniel wasn't with her anymore. Somewhere between their starting their pancakes and his getting up from the table, he'd drawn a shutter down over his feelings. She'd felt it, and couldn't help wondering if he regretted what had happened between them. Perhaps Daniel now thought their friendship had been compromised.

Or maybe it hadn't been what he'd expected. Maybe, while last night had more than lived up to her expectations, it hadn't been the same for him.

Nope. That doesn't feel right. What happened between us was too...incandescent. Incredible. Beautiful.

So she sat silently in his pickup, waiting for him to say something, until they were in front of her motel on Sweet Briar Street.

"Well." She shot him a smile, and wondered what he would do if she reached over and shook his hand. "Well." She got out of the truck, slammed the door, then walked steadily toward the motel entrance, trying not to stumble and fall as tears blurred her vision. If she'd known that making love to Daniel would destroy their friendship, she would have kept those fantasies in her head where they belonged.

"Meg." He caught her arm and then turned her, so her cheek came to rest against his shirtfront. "Meg," he whispered, his voice rough.

"Yes?" She desperately hoped her nose wouldn't run, because she didn't want to reveal her upset state of mind to him by wiping her nose.

He hesitated, and it seemed to her he was searching for words. Then he turned and, his arm around her shoulder, guided her toward the motel.

"Which room?"

"Number twelve."

He took the key out of her hand, unlocked the door, gently nudged her inside. And all the time she wondered what he was thinking.

Or regretting.

Well, as far as she was concerned, a faint heart never got anyone a darn thing.

"Daniel," she said shakily as she crossed the room and reached for a tissue. "Do you regret what happened?"

The expression in his gray eyes was absolutely incredulous. She had her answer, and the tight, constricted feeling in her chest started to ease.

"No." But he looked as cornered as a calf awaiting a branding. And suddenly, with feminine intuition, she felt only compassion for him. Emotions in the Willett family had never come easily—especially after Bob Willett had passed away.

"Okay." She blew her nose, tossed the tissue aside, then went over to him and threw her arms around him, hugging him tightly.

HE'D NEVER FELT anything so good.

And he felt awkward and inept, realizing how she had to be feeling. While he'd been driving, trying to find a way to put his emotions into words, she'd been pretty miserable. And it was all his fault.

"Meg," he whispered against her hair. And he'd

never been so content in his life, just holding her. She fit right into his arms as if she'd belonged there forever. And he didn't have a single doubt that he loved her and wanted her in his life forever. Yet he still didn't know if what he had to offer her was enough.

So he simply held her, for long, silent moments. Only when she eased her grip on him, ever so slightly, did he do the same and step back.

"I don't regret a thing," he said, looking down at her. He lifted a hand and stroked her hair, the side of her face. He skimmed a knuckle over her cheekbone, then smiled down at her.

"Me, either," she whispered.

"So," he said, taking his nerve in both hands. "You going to that dinner dance tonight?"

"Uh-huh."

"Would you like some company?"

Her blue eyes were shining, her mouth curved into a smile. "I'd love some."

"What time?"

"Maybe around six? They're taking a class picture before we go inside and eat."

"I'll be here."

And as Daniel walked back to his truck, he was a grateful man.

THERE WAS ONLY ONE thing she had to do before tonight's dinner dance, and that was to settle things with Heather and Laura. So Meg didn't waste any time. She changed clothes swiftly, into a pair of cutoffs, sneakers and a bright pink sweatshirt, then grabbed the keys to her rental car and headed toward Laura's house.

Laura lived just off Main Street, in a row of houses that fronted one of the lakes surrounding the town of Blue Spruce. Her grandmother had died and left her the house, and Laura had spent a lot of time and effort refurbishing the place. It had proved to be a real sanctuary during her divorce.

As Meg pulled up and parked her car in Laura's driveway, she had to admit that she admired what her friend had done with her life. At first, Laura had bounced around, through two years at a local college, followed by a disastrous marriage that lasted almost four years. During her divorce, her grandmother had died and left her the lakeside property and a small sum of money. Laura had then proceeded to rebuild her life from the ground up. She'd worked like a dog and put herself through beauty school.

Now, Laura's salon, The Cut 'n Curl, occupied the first floor of her large, Victorian-style house, and a generous porch wrapped around its front.

Laura loved wicker and green plants, crocheted afghans, hand-stitched quilts and fresh flowers. She not only maintained the hair salon, but also offered a four o'clock tea every Sunday afternoon. Her salon was one of the major places women gathered in Blue Spruce.

Laura had designed it that way. "My mission in life," she'd once told Meg over the phone, "is to help women realize how beautiful they are. And not just superficially. On the inside."

The house had a charming, turn-of-the-century look to it. Meg took her time strolling up the walkway, admiring the pansies, peonies and rosebushes blooming profusely on either side of the stone path.

Then she headed up the steps and inside the front door. A bell tinkled gently, and several feminine heads turned her way as she entered the sunlit salon.

"Hey!" Minnie Olsen, the manicurist, a mouse of a girl with soft brown hair and slightly scared eyes, smiled and stood. "Meg, it's good to see you!"

"Hey." Meg walked over to the thin girl and gave her a hug. Minnie blushed, but seemed pleased.

"I love your nails," Meg said.

Minnie was known all over Blue Spruce for her nail designs—the more outrageous the better. Today, a vivid purple shade adorned her fingernails, with a glittery golden overlay.

"Pikes Peak-a-Boo Purple, with Gold Digger's Delight as a topcoat. But I think I'm going to redo them before the banquet tonight. Maybe Pueblo Plum or Grand Teton Topaz." Minnie looked at her hopefully. "Do you need a manicure before tonight, Meg? I can work you in."

"Nope." She instinctively stuck her hands in the pockets of her cutoffs. They were working hands, more accustomed to pounding the keys on her laptop computer than soaking in a manicurist's bowl. "Actually, I came to see Laura."

"Oh, she's upstairs. With Heather." Minnie's face was a study in concern. "She has a headache. A real bad one. She's not feeling too good."

I'll bet.

"Then I'll just sneak on up and say hello quickly."

"Oh, she said she was going to rest—"

Meg laid a hand on the younger woman's arm.

"She's expecting me, Minnie. I'm sure she'd be disappointed if I didn't go on up."

"Oh. Okay. Oh, and I wanted to tell you, I think you have the most exquisite taste. That chandelier in the main hallway of your mansion—"

Meg bit the inside of her lip as Minnie went on, then mentally counted to ten before she started up the stairs toward Laura's living quarters.

She didn't have to search for her friend for long. Both Laura and Heather were in the main, master bedroom, which faced the street. Laura, in her brass bed, was huddled beneath a blue, gray and rose granny-square afghan, a wet washcloth on her forehead. Heather anxiously flitted about the large room.

They both started nervously as Meg stepped through the doorway.

Again, silence.

"C'mon, guys, I'm not that mad." Meg tried again. "It's not something that's worth getting that worked up about."

"I just feel awful," Laura moaned. "Both of us knew how hard it was for you to come back—"

"And then we go and do something so stupid—" Heather chimed in.

"And now you have to face our entire class tonight," Laura added.

"And they're probably going to give you the award for most successful or something—" Heather said.

Meg hadn't considered this.

How appropriate. The fraud comes home and gets an award. True irony. It would be beautiful in a novel, but it sure stinks in real life.

"Okay, fine. I'll let them give me an award, and I'll quietly give it back to Susie and Kevin before I leave. I'll tell them the truth, just like I will everyone else."

Meg had already decided she wasn't going to go into agonizing detail concerning her career lows. Even if she couldn't unload her second novel, she was proud to have sold her first. She just wanted to set the record straight about how and where she lived, and what the exact level of her financial success was.

"Why can't you think of it this way?" Heather asked. "By Blue Spruce standards, you *are* the most successful. Just by getting your novel published."

"That's a real achievement," Laura said hopefully, opening her eyes and peeking out from beneath the protective covering of the light blue washcloth.

"It's not gonna work, guys," Meg said softly.

They all stared at each other, then Meg walked slowly into the room. She removed a large brown teddy bear from the rocking chair by the window and sank down into the comfortable seat, the bear in her lap.

"I came back to put a few ghosts to rest," she said, meeting both her friends' anxious gazes. "And I can't return to Los Angeles leaving a bunch of lies behind me."

Laura started to cry. Meg got up, set the teddy bear back in the rocking chair, then sat down on the bed next to her friend, taking her hand.

"It's not like we didn't try to tell the truth," Laura began, hiccuping on a sob.

"I know," Meg said. "I know how rumors can get started in Blue Spruce. And how they can spread."

"They want to believe, Meg," Heather said. "Just thinking about your life makes Minnie happy."

"One of my customers said, 'At least someone got out of town and made her dreams come true,'" Laura added. "I don't think you understand what you mean to people here."

Meg hadn't considered this. Now she knew she had to speak straight from the heart, about how she really felt, from that most authentic place inside her. Otherwise, nothing good would be accomplished, and they would keep going around in the same circles.

"I guess the only way I feel bad is that...the whole thing kind of isolates me. It makes me feel different. On the outside again."

Laura's tears brimmed over once again. "I knew that would happen. And I knew how much it used to hurt you in high school. Oh, Meg, we're so sorry!"

Meg knew they were telling the truth. Heather and Laura were two of her dearest friends in the world. They knew all about how she had clashed with her mother, wanting nothing more than to simply fit in with the people of the small, Colorado town. But Antonia Prescott had always considered herself above what she so cuttingly referred to as "the masses," and had tried to instill in Meg a sense that she was better than anyone else.

Now, ten years after her high-school graduation, that sense of isolation haunted Meg still.

"I'll pick a good time to come clean," she said, trying to lighten the mood. "I'll make sure people understand it was nobody's fault—"

The phone rang. Laura quickly blew her nose, then reached for the receiver.

"Hello? Hi, Susie! Yeah, I'm getting ready for tonight. Wouldn't miss it. Meg? I know she's coming. What? A special award?"

Meg closed her eyes and counted to ten again.

"Sure, I— You know, Susie, why don't we go a little easy on the awards tonight? I think that Meg would want— No, I think she'd still realize how proud we are of her— No, I don't think that— Oh. You drove into Denver to get it specially made?"

Meg lowered her face into her hands.

"I guess— I think— Of course, Susie. I'm sure Meg will be happy. No, I won't tell her. A surprise. Of course."

Heather walked around behind Meg and she felt her friend's hand come down reassuringly on her shoulder.

"Yes, I know. I'm so proud of her, too. Well, I'll see you and Kevin tonight, then. Yeah. Yeah. Bye."

Laura hung up the phone, then closed her eyes and took a deep breath. Taking the washcloth off her forehead, she glanced up at Meg.

"Were you planning on telling everyone tonight?"

Meg considered what to do. It would be highly dramatic—not to mention effective—to tell everyone at the formal dinner tonight. On the other hand, she didn't think she had the guts—or the heart—to squash everyone's fantasies so ruthlessly.

"Not tonight. But I have to come clean before I leave."

"Perhaps as you board the plane," Heather suggested.

"Yeah," Meg said. "Dodging tomatoes all the way."

The three of them finally laughed.

ON THE WAY BACK to his ranch, Daniel thought about the concept of courtship.

Even in Blue Spruce, things had changed. There were more and more men and women who simply lived together, who drifted in and out of relationships with a casualness he found unappealing. And as he thought of all this, Daniel realized he wanted to do something to make Meg realize how much she meant to him.

She might not stay, but he wanted her to know how he felt.

He might not be able to put it into words, but perhaps his actions could speak for him.

With his decision made, he headed toward Betty's Floral Delights, on the corner of Main and Third. The small shop, with an extensive greenhouse attached, was located near the local grocery store, and he had no trouble parking and walking into the nursery.

Betty Bickham, in her late sixties and the mother of seven, had opened the nursery with her husband's help after her youngest had flown the coop. With one of the greenest thumbs Daniel knew, she'd always shown both common sense and compassion. He knew he could rely on her for help.

Several of Meg's classmates were in the shop when he walked in, the men picking up corsages they'd ordered, the women looking as if they would like to be given flowers. When Betty shot Daniel a questioning glance as she carefully packaged an elegant wrist corsage for a waiting customer, he shook his head and simply wandered around the extensive greenhouse.

Once they were alone, he approached her counter.

"What can I do for you, Daniel?" Betty asked. She was a tall, angular woman, with a strong face and hazel eyes. Her hair, a soft shade of gray, was pulled back from her face in a neat twist. Today she was dressed in a blue-gray sweatshirt, denim overalls, and red hightops.

"Flowers for a very special woman. Something romantic. Something a woman would want."

Betty considered this. "What's she like?"

"She laughs a lot. Always looking on the bright side. Very smart."

"And you're head over heels."

"Yep." He didn't mind admitting the truth to her. In his heart of hearts, Betty Bickham was the mother he'd always wanted—strong, steady and compassionate.

"If she were a flower—"

"A daisy. But—"

"I understand. You want something for her besides daisies."

"Yeah."

"Well." Betty considered this. "The way I see it, even the daisies I've known have liked to see themselves as roses. Do you get my drift?"

"I think I do."

"Now we just have to decide what color."

"What do you think?" Suddenly he felt unsure again.

"Let's have a look."

Her roses were glorious. Yellow and white, salmon and pink, deep rich red and an almost-purple shade that took his breath away.

"I'm over my head here, Betty."

She smiled. "If I were you, I'd go for the classic dozen. Deep red. Terrific fragrance. Their scent will fill her entire room."

He took great pleasure at the thought of there being something in Meg's motel room that would make her think of him. The only thing that would make him any happier was if he was in the room with her.

"All right."

"Some greenery, of course."

He nodded.

"And one daisy, in the middle of the entire bunch."

That stopped him.

"She knows you think of her as a daisy?"

He thought back to their past together, to the one other time he'd given her flowers. He'd picked a bunch of wildflowers and given them to her one afternoon when she'd been depressed. Alec told him later that she'd kept them until they were dried, brown stalks.

"I think so."

"Gives it a little something special," Betty said as she reached for one perfect daisy. "Upsets the balance a little, if you know what I mean."

Daniel pulled out a few bills as Betty readied the bouquet. He paid for his purchase, including the small delivery fee.

"Where to?"

"The Aspen Motel, on Sweet Briar."

"Room number?"

"Twelve."

He saw her smile as she took this information down.

"Name."

He hesitated.

"Couldn't be Meg Prescott now, could it? I heard that little girl was back in town."

The gaze she gave him was fond, so he didn't mind that she'd guessed.

"Yep."

"I'm glad to hear it."

Mercifully, she didn't say anything more. He thanked her, then strode out to his truck, immensely pleased with himself.

BETTY WATCHED HIM GO, leaning her elbows on the counter. She didn't take her eyes off Daniel until his truck left the parking lot, then she sighed and studied the bouquet she'd just created.

"It's about time, Daniel Willett. It's about time."

5

MEG ENDED UP EATING a late lunch with Laura and Heather, on the back porch of Laura's house. They sat at one of the tables usually used for Laura's Sunday teas and watched the surface of the lake shimmer in the afternoon sunlight.

Over chicken salad with mango chutney, green beans from the garden, and homemade lemonade, Meg attempted to reassure Laura that all was not lost.

"I'll accept the award," she said, taking another sip of lemonade and leaning back in her wicker chair. "But I won't take it back to Los Angeles with me. I think...I may stay a little longer than I'd planned. Another week. That'll give me time to have lunch with Susie and explain how the whole thing got out of control."

"Blame us entirely," Laura said, pushing some of her chicken salad around on the rose-patterned china plate. Her gaze drifted to Heather, in the garden out back, cutting roses and arranging a bouquet.

"I don't blame you," Meg said, wanting to put her friend at ease. "It could've happened to anyone. Besides, we had so much fun on that vacation."

Laura had to smile at that, then her expression grew pensive. "I admire you, Meg."

"How?" She was curious.

"Because you still have the capacity to...embrace

life." Laura fiddled with the petal of a peony, part of the bouquet of flowers she'd placed on their lunch table. "You stayed with Daniel overnight. Even if nothing happened, you were able to trust him."

Meg knew that even four years later, Laura had trouble with the idea of ever being with a man again. Her divorce had been a disaster. Everyone in Blue Spruce had known about Jack and the barmaid he'd run off with. Laura had loved him. His betrayal had devastated her.

"Daniel and I have been friends for years."

"Have you ever wondered what would happen if the two of you crossed that line? What it would be like to sleep with him?"

"Sure." She mentally crossed her fingers at the glaring omission she was making concerning her relationship with Daniel. But she just wasn't ready to talk about it yet. She'd been thinking about him constantly, all day, ever since he'd dropped her off at the motel. And she'd wondered what would happen tonight, after the dinner dance at the country club.

She knew what she wanted to have happen. She could only hope Daniel wanted the same thing.

Laura sighed. "You've been away too long, Meg. I don't think you really understand what you mean to this town. Especially the women. Most of us wish we could have gone after that brass ring instead of an engagement ring. Been as adventurous as you. But we're not. I'm not."

"Give yourself time. The great healer. You'll be embracing life in no time."

"It's been a couple of years, Meg. I don't know if I'm going to be able to pull myself out of this slump."

"I have faith in you."

"I'm glad someone does."

Meg shaded her eyes and glanced out into the garden. "What about Heather?"

"She's dating a guy she met on-line about eight months ago. He comes out from Denver on weekends."

"Nice guy?"

"*Very* nice." Now Laura sounded wistful.

Meg reached over and caught her friend's hand. She knew that although Laura had achieved so much, her real dream—the quiet one she held close to her heart—was to find a man and create a family with him. There was no one she knew who deserved the fulfillment of that dream more.

"Laura, there's someone in the world who's perfect for you, and when you're ready, he'll show up."

Laura smiled at that. "Your mother should have named you Sunny."

Meg leaned back in her chair and grinned. "Sunny Prescott. Hmm. I can see that on the cover of a book."

They both laughed.

SHE ARRIVED BACK AT her motel, opened her door, and immediately saw the roses. A deep, quiet pleasure filled her, for she knew they had to be from Daniel.

Dumping her shoulder bag on the queen-size bed, she reached for the small white card tucked among the green ferns and leaves.

Daniel.

Just his name. And not his handwriting. No message. She bit her lip, studied the card, and wondered.

The Daniel she'd known in high school had been a young man of few words. He'd been quiet in class, made excellent grades, and left shortly after the school day was over. The only place she'd really seen him open up was at the Willett ranch, and then only after she'd gotten to know his entire family, through Bob Willett.

Daniel was a lot like his father, she realized. Bob hadn't been a terribly talkative man, but he'd always managed to say the right words at the perfect moment. Meg had leaned on him twice during her high-school years, when dealing with her mother had proved more than she could handle. Their long talks in the barn had helped her to understand her mother, and to find direction in her own life.

Now she recognized the same quiet strength in Daniel that she'd so admired and come to love in his father.

She studied the card again.

Daniel.

She smiled, slowly recognizing the glorious bouquet for the huge step it was. And then she saw the white daisy, nestled amid the perfect, deep-red buds.

How like Daniel, to remember she loved wildflowers above all others. She thought back to the bouquet he'd picked for her that summer. She'd placed it in a vase in the window of her room overlooking Main Street, and kept it there until the flowers had withered into crisp brown stalks.

Her mother, rummaging through her room on some pretext or other, had seen them and thrown them out.

Meg had pressed two of the flowers before the entire bouquet had been trashed, and still had them in the pages of one of her journals. She'd never confronted her mother about what she'd done, as she'd intuitively sensed the woman's deep uneasiness over her relationship with Daniel.

With all the Willett boys.

"Simply unsuitable," Antonia had said more than once.

Meg had merely continued to eat her dinner, or read her book, or attend to her homework. Toward the end of her time in Blue Spruce, the last two years of high school, she'd simply ignored her mother's standards and demands, choosing to be out of the house as much as possible. Despite her mother's objections, she'd gotten a part-time job in town. Not as much for the money as for a peaceful place to go after school.

She'd done nothing to aggravate her mother, simply recognized that although they were related by blood, they could have been from two different planets when it came to what each of them considered to be important.

Then, shortly after graduation, she'd taken the money she'd squirreled away in Blue Spruce's bank— the five hundred from the sale of that short story along with countless paychecks from the two years she'd worked at Murphy's Drugstore—and hit the road.

She'd never looked back. And had never taken a dime from her mother, although she forced herself to call Antonia every two weeks, on Sunday, for exactly ten minutes. Whether she wanted to or not. Whether Antonia wanted to hear from her or not.

They were usually the longest ten minutes of her life.

The one concession she'd made to wanting her mother's approval had been when her novel was released. Now, in retrospect, Meg considered that moment to have been sheer foolishness, but a weakness that she considered understandable.

The day she'd received her author's copies in the mail, she'd slipped one into a padded envelope and addressed it to her mother, to that sleek, modern apartment in Manhattan.

The following Sunday, when she'd dutifully called, no reference had been made to receiving it. She still didn't know whether her mother had even read it—although she'd probably thoroughly looked over, and criticized, the photo on the inside flyleaf. And shuddered at the sight of Sluggo, tongue lolling out, snuggled happily in Meg's arms.

Snap out of it. This is getting depressing.

Meg walked over to the large window and slid the curtains open. Late-afternoon sunlight washed the room, and she moved the bouquet to the table in front of the window, so the brilliant red roses and single white daisy blazed to life in the sunlight.

Better.

She had more important things to worry about. Like a dinner dance tonight with Daniel. Like knocking his socks off when he arrived at six.

Like spending another night with him. And somehow managing to tell him how much she cared.

HE ARRIVED OUTSIDE her door promptly at six, a little nervous. Full of anticipation. At his knock, she answered the door, and he stepped inside, immediately seeing the bouquet on the table by the window.

Then, when he looked at her, he found he couldn't think.

She looked—stunning. Meg, dressed in a little black dress, her diamond earrings sparkling, her heels impossibly high, simply silenced him.

"You look very handsome," she said, and he forced himself back to the present and out of the thoughts that had been racing through his head—most of them revolving around how quickly he could get her out of that dress once tonight's dinner was officially over.

And suddenly he was glad he'd taken the time to wash his truck, to carefully clean it inside and out. It was bad enough that he had to take Meg to her reunion in one of the ranch's utility vehicles, but it would have to do. He felt like an unskilled rube, not having had the foresight to rent a car, something more in keeping with the occasion.

At least he'd dressed the part. The dark suit was one he rarely wore, but it still fit and was of a timeless, classic style.

"Thank you. Meg, you look...wonderful."

"Thanks."

Wonderful. Such a lame word, compared to what he felt when he looked at her. She simply sparkled. And there was something different about her tonight. He couldn't quite figure out what it was, but he meant to try.

"Your hair... It's different."

"Do you like it?"

"Yes."

She leaned forward and whispered in his ear. "Less mousse. Less attitude."

"Ahh." Her perfume, a spicy scent, had wafted up around him, and he found himself breathing deeply, taking in her fragrance, her warmth.

"I've decided I'm probably going to sweat a few things out tonight, so I thought I'd go au naturel."

And he understood. Her face looked different, as well. Less makeup. A lighter lipstick. More...*vulnerable*, for lack of a better word.

"What are you scared of tonight, Blue?" The words were out of his mouth before he could restrain them. Something was bothering her, and he wanted to help.

He sensed her hesitation. "Nothing. Not with you by my side." She linked her arm through his and smiled up at him. "And thanks for the corsage. How did you know white orchids are another of my favorites?"

He had no idea what she was referring to, but kept his expression carefully bland. She was already heading toward the small, built-in refrigerator in the corner of the large motel room, and now retrieved the clear box containing a corsage. Three small white orchids, festooned with shiny, purple-and-white satin ribbon, Blue Spruce High School's team colors.

Betty. You sly dog.

The older woman was obviously trying to help their romance along, and Daniel was grateful. But he wondered how he would manage to keep his hands steady when he pinned the orchids onto her dress.

She solved the problem for him. "I love wrist corsages more than the other kind," she said, slipping the slender band over her hand. "Don't you?"

He wouldn't have known the difference.

"It looks beautiful on you, Blue."

Her smile practically lit up the room. "Thank you, Daniel. It was so thoughtful. And romantic."

He locked the door after her as they headed out into the early-summer evening. And silently thanked Betty for getting their night off to such a good start.

HANDLEMAN'S COUNTRY Club had been done up for the occasion, with purple-and-white balloons and computer-generated banners announcing the reunion, along with the sign outside by the highway: Welcome, Class Reunion.

Once inside, Meg was hustled away from Daniel, and he watched as the class picture was set up. Shot after shot was taken, as each time someone in the class of two hundred and eighty complained of closing their eyes or not smiling. Hoots of laughter and good-natured teasing floated out over the soft evening air.

"Last one!" Wilbur Granacki, the town photographer, warned. In Daniel's eyes, Wilbur had always reminded him of the scarecrow in *The Wizard of Oz*. Strangely, he didn't seem to have aged much over the years. But he did excellent work, and Susie and Kevin Brackman had been wise to hire his services.

"Put Meg up front!" someone yelled.

Daniel watched as Meg demurred, but various class members were insistent. Finally she walked to the front of the group and knelt down in the grass, beneath the large stand of blue spruce trees. Wilbur had provided a cloth runner for those in the front row to kneel on, and now Meg faced front and center.

"Big smile!" Wilbur called. The camera clicked several times, then he signaled he was finished for the evening.

"Everybody inside!" Susie called, flushed and glowing from the excitement. "If I can't tempt you all with prime rib, I don't know what's gonna work!"

Good-natured laughter met this announcement, and Daniel walked out onto the thick, plush lawn in search of Meg. He found her, talking to one of her classmates, who apparently had a daughter who wanted to make writing her career.

He listened as Meg gave the woman very practical, well-thought-out advice, including advising her daughter to take a few semesters of computer classes and learn how to type. She also reached inside her tiny, black-beaded evening bag and took out a card. He realized she was giving the woman her home phone number in Los Angeles.

"If Mindy has any questions, just tell her to give me a call. Evenings are best for me."

Then he took her arm, so proud to have her by his side, and escorted her indoors.

THE BUFFET STAGGERED the imagination. Prime rib, along with garlic-mashed potatoes and brown gravy. A salad bar with every chopped-up vegetable and dressing imaginable, and several hot vegetable dishes. Three different types of bread, an open bar, and a separate table groaning beneath the weight of six different desserts—three of them chocolate.

In the middle of the dessert table was a huge sheet cake whose iced surface welcomed home Blue Spruce

High's classmates with elaborate, swirling letters drawn in rich, butter-cream frosting.

Susie and Kevin had outdone themselves, Daniel thought, as he stayed close behind Meg in the serving line. He listened as she chatted with each of the servers. While a few of the men in front of them had simply grunted and pointed to the food they wanted, Meg carried on a complete conversation with each and every uniformed employee. Daniel loved the way she loved people, and how genuinely interested she was in each of their lives.

He almost laughed out loud when, instead of having to choose between the mushroom Burgundy gravy and the creamed horseradish sauce to accompany the beef, the server offered Meg both, "Because you just have to try them."

"Thank you, Eduardo," she'd said, then turned, plate in hand, to wait for Daniel.

Eduardo, clearly figuring out that the two of them were together, offered Daniel the same choice, which he eagerly accepted. Then he moved to Meg's side, and they scanned the huge room—a veritable sea of white tables surrounding the dance floor in the candlelit ballroom—for a place to sit.

"Over here!" he heard, and turned to see Susie waving, indicating they should join them.

"All right with you?" he asked Meg, and she nodded.

They were soon joined by Heather and her date from Chicago, Donald, then another couple who were close friends of Susie and Kevin.

"I'm so glad we got you at this table," Susie said,

touching Meg's arm lightly, her face glowing. "I can't wait to have you tell us all about life in the fast lane!"

"Honey, let her eat first," said Kevin, the ever-practical husband.

"Oh, I know. But I don't want Meg getting away before I hear all about Los Angeles."

Daniel sensed a quiet tension building in Meg, and reached beneath the table for her free hand. He found it, held it, squeezed it, and was rewarded by the look of relief and gratitude she sent him. His touch seemed to soothe her, and he held her hand for just a minute before letting it go and starting to work on his dinner.

He listened much more than joined in the conversation. After all, he wasn't really part of this class reunion, having graduated two years earlier. Also, most people in town knew what he was up to, that he was working the property his father had left the family. The star at the table was Meg, and he wanted her to shine. So Daniel quietly ate his prime rib and watched her.

Nervous. Electric and nervous. And jumpy. Those would have been his first impressions of her. Although her eyes were bright and she smiled constantly, he caught the slight sense of desperation. She'd seemed so much more relaxed alone with him at the ranch.

Now, she was barely able to eat two mouthfuls in a row before someone at the table asked her a question, or someone else came by to tell her how much they'd enjoyed reading her novel.

She was a bona fide star; the only star Blue Spruce had ever produced. And Daniel could see the town was proud of Meg. Proud of what she'd become, and elated by the fact that she'd chosen to come back home.

"So, out of everything," Kevin said later, over coffee and dessert, "what is it you like the most about Los Angeles? The earthquakes or the smog?"

"Honey!" Susie said, admonishing her husband. She turned to Meg. "He just thinks he's a little more worldly than the rest of us, because his company once flew him out to Anaheim for a computer conference."

"Yeah, and she never forgave me for not taking her with me and letting her see Disneyland," Kevin said, grinning.

"I've only felt one earthquake, and it was a doozy," Meg said. "The smog comes and goes. It's not too bad in the winter." She paused. "I have to think about this one a minute."

"Take your time," Heather said.

Daniel rested his arm along the back of Meg's chair. He could still feel the tension humming inside her, and wondered about its source. It was so clear to him that her classmates adored her, even looked up to her. She'd left town on a grand adventure, had gone to conquer the world, and had succeeded. In his opinion, if the only thing she ever produced was that first novel, it was more than most people contributed to their community—or to the planet—in a lifetime.

"Okay," Meg said, having polished off both a piece of chocolate cake and part of a slice of Mud Pie. "I think what I love the most is that the city never sleeps. The first few years I was there, I loved walking into bookstores at any hour, talking with people, having a cup of coffee. So much information, so much opportunity. The classes available, the way everyone in the city was trying to do something. Acting, writing, music—

you name it. There was always something going on. Something to do. Something to learn."

And Daniel thought of the day he'd driven into Denver and found her book. How uncomfortable he'd been in the bookstore with the small café attached. How he would no sooner have sat down and relaxed over a *caffe latte* and almond *biscotti* than he would have given his Arabians their breakfast off a fine china plate.

He was a stranger to Meg's world, and knew it. But as he listened to her create Los Angeles for the people at their table and share her sense of adventure with them, he wondered if he would be more comfortable in that world if he explored it with her.

Or would he embarrass her?

He couldn't bear the thought of that. Taking a long swallow of his coffee, Daniel forced himself to listen to the conversation at the table and not go off into his own private thoughts.

People laughed. Asked questions. More classmates stopped by. Soon it was evident that the place to be this evening was at this particular front table, with Meg. Daniel felt her reach toward him, beneath the table, searching for his hand again.

Then the band started to vamp to the song, "Beat It," and the crowd around the table dispersed. The band's lead singer welcomed everyone back, and said they were there to play classic rock songs to help everyone travel further down memory lane.

"So, right now," the lead singer said, pointing out into the darkened audience, "I want you and you, and you, too, over there, to go get that girl who got away, the one you really wanted to ask out, and take her out on the dance floor. Let tonight be a night for memories, 'cause we'll be playing lots of songs about those memories."

The drummer counted off the beat, and the band launched into a slow, soothing rendition of the Beatles' "Yesterday."

Daniel squeezed Meg's hand. "Dance?"

"I'd love to."

He led her out onto the dance floor, thinking that in all the time he'd known Meg, they'd never danced together. Several other couples joined them, and although the floor wasn't crowded, they were far from isolated.

He tried not to hold her too closely, but he wanted to. If he'd had his way, he would have slung her over his shoulder and carried her out to his truck, then spirited her off to his ranch. He'd had just about enough of sharing Meg this evening, even though he knew it was her time to shine. She certainly deserved it.

"You okay?" he asked.

"Now I am."

She snuggled closer, resting her cheek trustingly on his shirtfront, and he simply gave in and held her as closely as he wanted to. Oh, the phone lines in Blue Spruce would be burning up tonight if the curious looks he was receiving were any indication. But right now, Daniel didn't care. It just felt too right, and far too good, having Meg in his arms.

Slowly, as he held her close while they danced, he felt the tension leave her body. Then another kind of tension replaced it, and he found himself looking down into her blue eyes and seeing his feelings about how he wanted this evening to end mirrored in her expression.

"How soon do you want to leave?" she asked, and his heart sped up, started into overdrive.

"As soon as you want to."

"Just a little longer, then," she said, and they continued to dance, as one slow song segued into the next.

After they'd danced through three songs, they returned to the table to find Heather sitting alone, a worried expression on her face.

"Laura didn't show," she whispered as Daniel pulled out a chair for Meg.

"What?"

"I've been looking for her, and then I asked Susie. She wasn't here for the class picture, and no one's seen her."

"Oh, no." Meg glanced up at Daniel, and he saw the worried expression in her eyes. "We've got to find her."

"You've got to stick around and get that award, or Susie will be heartbroken," Heather whispered. Then she leaned back and seemed to be trying to compose herself as her date, Donald, the computer expert from Denver, rejoined the table.

"Did you call her?" Meg whispered to Heather. Daniel could barely hear what she'd said.

Heather nodded. "No answer."

Meg turned toward Daniel and took his hand.

"What do you want to do?" Daniel asked. "What do you want me to do?"

"I'm worried about her. She was acting depressed the last time I saw her."

"Could you ask Susie to hold off on the award until we go to Laura's house and check up on her?" he said.

"The only problem is, she doesn't know that I know about it. I was at Laura's when she called and told her." Briefly, she told him about the specially made award that Susie had driven into Denver to collect.

"Sit here for just a second," he said, giving her hand a squeeze. "I think I have a solution."

He got up from the table, scanned the room, then found Susie by the dessert table, talking with one of the servers.

"Susie," he said when he reached her side, "Meg's got a bit of a problem. We've got to go check on a friend, but we're definitely going to be back."

Susie's mouth rounded, then she bit her bottom lip. "Is it something serious?"

"We're not sure yet, but I don't think so. It's just something that has to be attended to right away."

"Oh." She considered this. "But you'll be back?"

"Within about ninety minutes, at the latest."

He could see her doing quick calculations in her mind. Probably timing when she would arrange for Meg to receive her special award.

"Okay. But give me a call if you're going to be any later than that, so I can adjust things."

"We will."

Back at the table, he leaned down and whispered, "Let's go."

"But I—"

"Everything's taken care of."

The look she gave him was worth any inconvenience.

"Thank you so much, Daniel." Now she was standing, and he put his arm around her waist as they headed toward the door.

"You aren't leaving?" Daniel recognized Minnie Olsen by her long, topaz-colored nails and incredibly short skirt as she grabbed hold of Meg's forearm. "You *can't!*"

"Just for a little while," Daniel said, gently disengaging the hold the woman had on Meg. And for the first time this evening, he saw how much pressure they'd all put on Meg. None of them would have deliberately hurt her, but they still demanded a lot from her. In a funny way, she represented all their dreams, and had become a symbol for this high-school class. Something that no single person could live up to.

Then they were out in the parking lot, searching for his truck. Once they found it, Daniel wasted no time in starting toward Laura's house. The upset expression on Meg's face made him pick up speed. He couldn't stand to see her this way.

"Anything else I can do?" he asked quietly as the truck sped along the highway toward town.

She took his hand then, gripping it tightly.

"Just stay with me, Daniel. Just be right here for me."

He lifted her hand to his lips, kissed the slender fingers, then concentrated on his driving.

Whatever she wanted or needed, he would be there.

6

THERE WASN'T A SINGLE light on in Laura's house. The large Victorian appeared eerily dark and abandoned as Daniel and Meg walked up the flagstone path toward the front porch. The flowers surrounding them seemed like part of a surreal garden, glinting white and silver in the moonlight.

Meg walked slightly ahead of Daniel and reached the steps before him. She leaped up them, anxious to get to her friend, and rapped sharply on the front door three times.

No answer.

Meg knocked again, a little louder this time, but she knew she wasn't going to get an answer. If Laura was inside, she'd already heard her and didn't want to talk. Meg didn't exactly have a bad feeling about this. She didn't think Laura was about to do anything drastic, but she knew her friend had to be in pain.

"Let's try the back door," she whispered to Daniel.

He nodded.

They walked across the generous porch, and around the house. But before either of them reached the back door, she saw Laura, sitting in one of the wicker chairs, her feet tucked up beneath her, her body snugly wrapped in an afghan. She was staring out at the lake as the moonlight danced on its shimmering surface.

"Hey, Laura." Meg sat down in the wicker chair across from her friend. Out of the corner of her eye, she saw Daniel sit in a chair farther back. How like Daniel, to know she had to approach Laura carefully and not embarrass her. She would assess her friend's mood and work from that point. She gained strength just knowing Daniel was there if she needed him.

"Hey." Laura continued to stare out over the lake, and Meg felt now was not the time to pry.

After a short and not entirely uncomfortable silence, Laura said, "I just couldn't do it, Meg."

"I know." Meg reached across and took her friend's hand, then gently squeezed her fingers.

"I couldn't go there tonight and smile and laugh and make believe that everything was okay—that my life was okay—when it's not, and I don't think it ever will be."

Meg knew that now was not the moment to tell Laura that time had a miraculous way of healing a person, of making someone see events in an entirely new light. She knew Jack hadn't been good enough for Laura, that he was simply a user. Would always be a user. Everyone in town had known this.

Everyone but Laura.

But Meg also knew there was a part of her friend who had taken the failure of her marriage very personally, as if it had been her fault and hers alone. Meg could understand how Laura had lost both heart and nerve and couldn't bear the thought of going to a class reunion and seeing all her classmates with their "perfect" lives. Spouses who didn't cheat on them. Children. Happy homes with love and laughter and the warm security that came from knowing you were surrounded by people who truly cared about you.

Meg could certainly understand. In one way, Laura had been a lot more honest than she had been. Or perhaps it was simply the fact that Meg hadn't been hurt as badly, and was able to be a bit more of an actress about her life.

Not publishing a second or third novel didn't hold a candle to having your heart broken.

"Hi, Daniel," Laura said suddenly. Quietly. "Thank you for bringing Meg here. I appreciate it."

"Am I making you uncomfortable by being here, Laura?"

"Nope. I have nothing to hide."

Meg wasn't quite sure what to do. She had no idea how to comfort her friend. They'd talked about the divorce a lot on the phone, and she'd known the best thing she could do was listen to Laura go over the story, again and again. Although Meg had wanted to say hateful things about Jack, she hadn't. He had been Laura's husband, and she was still in love with him.

So she'd listened, and offered comfort. Told Laura what a terrific person she was. Arranged for both Laura and Heather to come out to Los Angeles for that fateful vacation, using part of her advance to help them finance the plane tickets. And it had worked, because that week in Los Angeles had cheered Laura up and started her on the road to feeling a lot better about herself.

Frustrated now, Meg found she didn't know what to do. Couldn't find the words. No matter what she told Laura, no matter what an extraordinary woman she thought Laura was, what it all boiled down to was that her dear friend thought she was a failure. A big fat nothing.

She glanced at Daniel. He rose from his chair and approached Laura. Before she knew what he was up to, he'd sat down in the wicker chair on the other side of her friend.

"Sometimes when a man cheats on his wife, it has nothing to do with her," he said quietly. His voice sounded so soothing, Meg felt as if she could lean toward it and find comfort.

Laura looked up at him, her face in the moonlight so raw and open, so *hurting*, that Meg's throat tightened.

"I keep wondering what I did..." Her voice trailed off.

"Nothing," Daniel said. "No one could have helped Jack. There was a part of him that was driven."

Meg watched. Held her breath. Laura was looking at Daniel so intently, and Meg realized that while most of them had walked on eggs around Laura—and had for some time—Daniel was telling her the truth.

"That's...that's what it was like. What it felt like. Driven," Laura said.

Daniel nodded.

"Do you think..." Laura paused, then Meg almost felt the painful breath her friend slowly took in. "Daniel, do you think he ever loved me?"

"As much as he was capable of loving anyone."

As much as he was capable of loving anyone. With that one sentence, Meg was transported back to years ago, to a winter's day inside a warm barn on a ranch at the foot of the Rockies. To the father she'd wished had been her own. To being that sobbing teenage girl, her head against Bob Willett's broad, comforting shoulder.

And to the emotional common sense that had been passed down so lovingly from father to son.

As much as she is capable of loving anyone. Daniel's father had said the exact same words about her mother that day. He'd told her the truth, that moment in the barn, and, in a certain way, he'd saved her life in the process. He'd helped her face the reality of what a self-centered woman her mother had been and always would be. He'd stopped her denial, her hope that someday things would get better. Because that vain hope had been slowly destroying her.

And he'd also helped her find a way to deal with it and move on.

She blinked, and within a heartbeat was back in the present. And it was almost as if she were seeing Bob Willett come back to life, here on Laura's porch. Laura was sobbing, her cheek against Daniel's broad shoulder, and he was holding her, Meg knew, the same way his father had offered her comfort.

And she realized, at that exact moment, that the older man hadn't truly died, because he'd left a part of himself in Daniel. In all of his sons, but especially in Daniel.

He'll make a wonderful father.... And with that thought, the queerest little ache entered her chest.

When Laura finally stopped sobbing, she slowly let out another painfully drawn breath. "I just feel so...*ashamed.*"

"You have nothing to be ashamed of." Daniel was

looking at her now as she sat curled up in her chair. He'd drawn his own chair up close to Laura's.

"You really think so?"

"How is it ever wrong to love someone?"

Meg's eyes filled and she looked away. As soon as she could compose herself, she glanced back. Laura was actually laughing at something Daniel had said. He was smiling.

"So," said Laura, turning toward Meg. "Did you get that award?"

"Nope," Meg said carefully. Now she felt as if her emotions had just entered overdrive. "I have to get back and let Susie do her thing."

"Why don't you come with us?" Daniel suggested. Laura seemed astounded.

"Oh, but I—"

"You'll feel better," he said.

"I think Daniel's right," Meg said.

"If you—I guess I could—" Laura hesitated.

"The desserts are killer," Meg said, consciously trying to lighten the moment.

"I'll be really quick," Laura promised.

"We've got—" Daniel glanced at his watch "—exactly thirty-eight minutes. If you're ready in twenty, we can make it."

"Okay." Laura leaped up from her chair and disappeared inside her back door, the crocheted afghan flapping behind her. Brilliant light came on in the house as she headed toward the second floor.

Meg reached for Daniel's hand.

Oh, Daniel. Your daddy would have been so proud.

"AND FOR THE CLASSMATE who traveled the farthest, that award goes to Cynthia Wittenberg, who came all the way from Scotland!"

A round of heartfelt applause erupted as Meg, Daniel and Laura made their way into the back of the country club's ballroom. Meg watched as Daniel signaled to Kevin, who quickly sent a note to the podium up front, where Susie reigned as master of ceremonies.

Most Years Married and Most Children followed swiftly, as servers wheeled what remained of the giant cake onto the dance floor in the center of the ballroom. They made their way through the tables, encouraging attendees to have more of the decadent dessert, along with another cup of coffee for the road.

Daniel and the two women reached one of the tables in back and sat down. Meg glanced proudly at her friend. Laura looked terrific in a royal-blue beaded dress, her long red hair upswept in an elegant French twist. No one would have guessed that less than an hour ago, she'd been sobbing her heart out. All those semesters in beauty school certainly hadn't gone to waste. Laura looked radiant.

"We have a special award tonight," Susie began, and Meg felt Daniel's warm gaze on her. She gave him a small smile in return.

"It's a rare event when someone in any high-school class makes a mark for him- or herself in the world." Susie smiled out over the audience, and her expression seemed to be saying, *I saved the best for last.*

"I think we all knew that this particular classmate of ours was going to go out and set the world on fire. Not just Blue Spruce, but the *world.*"

Spontaneous applause broke out, and Susie waited until it died down.

"You all know who I'm talking about. Or if you don't, you must have been living in a cave for the last few years." She took a deep breath, and her sparkling black dress caught the spotlight and flashed brightly.

"I met Meg Prescott and got to know her the year we endured—I mean, *attended*—Mrs. Hecht's home-economics class."

Hoots of laughter greeted this statement, along with one irrepressible voice calling out, "*Loved* those blueberry muffins!"

Meg felt her body grow more tense with every word.

"I also sat next to her in choir, and I can tell you from experience, no one could make me laugh harder, or get me in more trouble, than Meg."

More laughter greeted her words. Susie waited patiently until it died down.

"But seriously, I don't think Meg has any idea how her presence tonight has affected us all. You see, when someone attains her exalted level of success, it's rare to find them coming back and remembering a town like Blue Spruce, or the people who live here."

Now the audience was silent. Listening.

"I read Meg's book," Susie continued. "And I loved it." She looked out over the audience. "I think Meg Prescott is a rare jewel, a very special person in this world. And it gives me great pleasure to ask her to come on up and accept the award for the Most Successful member of this high-school class."

The applause almost deafened Meg as she stood, her legs shaky. Her stomach felt as if it were about to come apart, like that piece of Mud Pie might find its way back up.

"Go get 'em, Meg."

It took her a second to register what Daniel had said.

"Stay right here," she whispered against his ear. "Please don't leave."

Then she started the long walk to the podium.

ONCE SHE GOT THERE, the spotlight blinded her. She had no idea what she said, but she embraced Susie and accepted what was actually a gorgeous award. It looked like an Oscar, but instead of a little bald-headed man, it was a graceful, gold-plated woman in a gown, quill pen in hand.

She felt lower than a skunk's belly.

The crush she encountered as she tried to get back to Daniel threatened to overwhelm her.

"Good one, Meg!"

"Way to go, Prescott!"

"You were always such a riot—"

"Glad to see you could make it!"

"That *mansion!*"

Then she saw Daniel, striding through the crowd, and the expression on her face must have revealed her true feelings, because he gave her a comforting smile. She relaxed, and for a moment was almost enjoying herself before she heard Paula's distinctive, hard, whining voice.

"I'm gonna give that little bitch a piece of my mind! Why does she get paid so much when—"

Meg shot Daniel a look that he understood immediately. Reaching her side, he grabbed her arm, then began to clear a swath of space through the crush of bodies on the dance floor. After a quick word with Laura, they headed toward the door and into the night.

THEY SAT IN HIS TRUCK, in the parking lot of The Aspen Motel. Meg had kicked off her high heels. Her award sat on the seat between them.

"So, do you make a habit of this?" Daniel asked.

She had to laugh. "Running out of high-school reunions? Ask me after the barbecue tomorrow—they say the third time's the charm."

"What's her problem?"

She knew Daniel was referring to Paula.

"She can't stand my success. You know, word around town is that she beats her husband, Al, into complete submission, so I didn't want to hang around and see what she had planned for me!"

He laughed at that, and she had to join in.

When their laughter died down, Meg sighed. "Daniel, why can't I just fit in?"

He gave her a long, level look. "That's what you aspire to? To be like everyone else?"

"You have to admit, it would be a little more restful."

He smiled, and her heart sped up.

"Naw. I like you just the way you are."

She gave him a look right back. *Now or never.*

"Me, too. You, I mean." She took a deep breath. "Would you like to come in?"

He seemed to hesitate, then finally said, "Yes."

HE COULDN'T POSSIBLY make love to her again.

She would be leaving after the reunion was over, to

go back to the West Coast and the life she'd carved out for herself. And if loving Meg and watching her leave had been hard the first time, it would be doubly hard now that he'd actually made love to her.

He hadn't expected that to happen either time. Both had been like moments out of time. They'd had a little too much to drink that Friday night. She'd taken off her clothes the first time; she'd been half-naked in his bed the second. Both times she'd instigated things.

The morning after their passionate night together, when he'd woken up with her in his arms, he'd known that he had to put a stop to it. He couldn't keep getting closer and closer to her, then turn around and watch her walk away.

And it wouldn't be fair to ask her to stay.

He was at an emotional impasse, and Daniel knew that no matter how much it hurt, he would do the right thing.

He unlocked the motel-room door for her, ushered her inside. It gave him great pleasure to watch the way she first went to smell her roses, then carefully took off her corsage. She nestled it back into the original box, and placed it in the small refrigerator. Daniel knew she would probably save the flowers, holding on to the sweetness of the memories as long as possible.

As he would.

She didn't pay half as much attention to the award, which she set on top of the large television set the second she entered the room and didn't give another glance. It almost seemed as if Susie's grand gesture had deeply embarrassed her.

He didn't ask. One thing he knew about Meg was that if she chose to tell him, it would all come out. Otherwise, he felt it was none of his business.

"Something to drink? I've got soda and juice." She indicated the refrigerator.

"No, I should...I should be going, Meg."

He saw the hurt in her eyes instantly and hated himself for putting it there. But he had to protect her. And himself. He had to be the strong one, and do what was best for both of them.

"I think I know why you're leaving."

That stopped him cold. He simply stared at her.

"You know I'm a fraud."

That stopped him colder. He had no idea what she was talking about.

"Tonight. That whole awards thing. Daniel, I don't know if you're aware of it, but there are some pictures that have been making the rounds in town—"

"I've heard."

"Well, it's all a bunch of lies."

"Meg—"

"None of it's true. None of it. I want you to know, because I can't bear the thought of lying to you, even inadvertently."

"Meg, I—"

"I saw what you did with Laura tonight, and you're such an honest man. And I'm not. Honest, I mean. Though I never meant to lie, and when Laura was taking those pictures, I had absolutely no idea—"

He had absolutely no idea what she was talking about.

"Meg—" He tried to break in, but she kept talking,

something about a hotel on Sunset Boulevard in Beverly Hills, and too little sleep, staying up too late, drinking tons of caffeine—

"And then Laura was still depressed over her divorce, so I thought, what if they both came out and we spent a week just having fun, it might jar her out of her depression—"

"Meg, you—"

"But it all went wrong, and the thing was, I had no idea what had happened until I came back to town several years later, and by that time—"

"Honey, please—"

"By that time, no one would *believe* me."

Then she horrified him completely by bursting into tears.

"Oh, honey." He did the only thing he knew to do. He took her into his arms and guided her toward the queen-size bed. He sat them both down on the edge, and kept his arms tightly wrapped around her as she curled into his lap and sobbed as if her heart were broken.

He'd never seen her this hurt. This vulnerable. He couldn't bear to see her feeling this way. Her pain was his, and he held on, waiting for the storm to abate. He still wasn't quite sure what was going on, what had happened. He only knew that whatever kind of help Meg needed, he would be there for her.

She quieted, then simply leaned against him, her arms still tightly around him, her breath still catching on an occasional hiccup.

"Daniel?"

"Hmm."

"Do you hate me?"

"No."

"Do you think I'm a fraud?"

"Nope."

She sighed. "Do you think I deserved that award?"

"Yep."

"You do?"

"It was a hell of a novel, Blue." He kissed her forehead, then eased her out of his arms. "I'm going to tuck you into bed. I think you'll feel better in the morning."

"I'm glad we talked," she whispered as he lowered the zipper on her little black dress. He averted his eyes at the sight of a slender black bra strap.

"Me, too." He didn't really know what they'd talked about, but it seemed to have helped her.

He eased the dress off her, and tried not to look at Meg, a vision of feminine sexuality in the black-lace bra and matching wisp of panties. The only other pieces of clothing she had on—if you could call them that—were thigh-high, sheer black stockings that seemed to stay up by themselves.

"Into your bed," he said quietly. The sooner he got that beautiful body beneath the covers, the better off he would be.

"Just a second." She turned away. Unhooked her bra. Tossed it.

His mouth went dry.

Then she sat on the edge of the bed and quickly peeled off her stockings.

This, Daniel decided, was true torture. As soon as he had her safely tucked in bed, he was out of here.

She slid beneath the sheets, seemed to relax, and—

"Ouch."

He was already halfway to the motel-room door when he heard her. "What?"

"Nothing."

"Meg?"

"It's okay, Daniel. It just happens when I'm under stress."

Now he couldn't leave her alone. Fool that he knew he was, he approached the bed. But the moment he saw the genuine pain in her bright blue eyes, all traces of sexual desire left him.

"Blue, what's wrong?"

"My neck, I— It's a crick, and— It hurts to move."

"What can I do?"

"Heat. There's a heating pad—"

Following her instructions, he unearthed a heating pad from the bottom of her suitcase and plugged it in. Carefully placing it beneath her neck on the pillow, he held her hand until he felt her relax.

"Much better." She sighed, then began to breathe deeply.

He sat for almost ten minutes in the overstuffed chair by the bed. When he thought she was asleep, he rose to leave.

"Cowboy?" she said, her voice so soft it broke his heart. "Why don't you want me?"

He sat back down in the chair as his legs gave out on him. Of all the questions she could have asked him, he wasn't prepared for that one.

"Blue, it's not that I don't... It's because I think... I'm not sure that I can explain...." He was floundering badly, not knowing how to express what he felt.

"It's complicated," she said softly.

"Yes," he said, grateful that she'd seen fit to help him out of the situation.

"And it has nothing to do with not wanting," she added.

"Yes."

"But it's difficult for you to talk about right now."

"Yes."

She seemed content with his answers, and he waited.

"Would you do me a favor, Daniel?"

"Anything."

"Would you just sleep with me tonight? Just sleep, I promise. I'm not in much shape for anything else."

He didn't even hesitate. "All right."

She didn't even open her eyes as he checked that the door was locked, then turned off all the lights but the one in the bathroom. He eased that door almost shut so only the thinnest slice of light illuminated the bedroom.

He'd already done a mental inventory in his head. The dogs and horses would be fine until the morning. There was a dog door that led inside the ranch house, but they would probably all sleep in the barn unless they heard his truck come up the gravel driveway. He'd left them plenty of water and dry food.

The horses had all been fed before he'd left to pick up Meg this evening, and as long as he woke up early and headed out to the ranch, there would be no problem with their being alone for the night.

The thought of sleeping with her in his arms brought him great pleasure. He wasn't crazy about the fact that the townspeople of Blue Spruce would see his black pickup truck parked outside Meg's motel all night long. He wanted to protect her from their gossip. But in the end, he found he really didn't care what anyone thought. The only thing that mattered was being with Meg.

He shed his clothes quickly, folded and stacked them on the chair by the bed. He slipped beneath the covers. Gently, so as not to hurt her neck, Daniel took her in his arms.

Again, that feeling of it all being so *right* assailed him. She smiled, although her eyes remained closed, and he knew that even with the heat, she was still in a certain amount of pain. He also sensed that his presence in her bed helped comfort her.

"I'm here, baby," he whispered. "You lean on me if you want to, okay?"

"Okay," she whispered back, and as he studied her face in the soft, indirect light from the bathroom, he could see how much of a strain the entire night had been for her.

Maybe, in her own way, she needs me.

And with that thought, and with his arms protectively around her, Daniel finally drifted off to sleep.

HE OPENED HIS EYES BEFORE SUNRISE, used to getting up early in the morning to attend to the animals. The motel room was still dark, save for the narrow shaft of light coming from the bathroom.

Daniel eased himself out of the queen-size bed, careful not to disturb Meg. The room was comfortably warm, so he walked naked to the bathroom, answered nature's call, then washed his hands and face.

Quietly, efficiently, he made coffee, using the coffee maker the motel provided and the excellent coffee Meg had brought. He poured himself a cup, then sipped it slowly as he looked down at Meg, sleeping peacefully.

He loved her so much it hurt. The pain came from deep in his gut. From the instinctual knowledge that no other woman would ever mean as much to him.

And she was leaving. Again.

Well, you sure didn't encourage her to stay.

He dismissed that thought immediately. He'd wanted Meg to run free, and she had. At that time, at the age of nineteen, he hadn't had anything to offer her but his love. Even now, at thirty, with his ranch at the foot of the Rockies, he wasn't sure he had enough to offer, or if he ever would.

So many facets of Meg remained a mystery to him.

She shifted in her sleep. The sheet dipped lower, exposing her perfect breasts. He felt his emotional answer in his body's response, swift and strong. It had always been that way with Meg. That was one aspect of their relationship he had no trouble with.

He took another sip of coffee. Tried to think rationally. To stay cool and unemotional.

And lost, as always.

Daniel set his coffee down and started toward the bed.

SHE'D BEEN DREAMING of him, of making love with Daniel, and then her dream had seemed to fuse with reality. Barely awake, she'd felt him slip his fingers beneath the elastic of her panties, slowly drag them down, following their path with kisses. And she'd been so relaxed, barely out of sleep and her erotic dreams.

He nudged her thighs apart, kissed her *there*, and that woke her up. The erotic sweetness of the gesture almost made her heart stop. Meg didn't hesitate; she merely entwined her fingers in his hair and held him, urged him on, let him have his way until her climax erupted, making her cry out and shake, then clutch him to her as he slid up her body and held her tightly.

He positioned himself above her and she welcomed him, sighing with pleasure at the exquisite sensation of being so completely filled. He moved inside her, thrusting strongly, and she answered those thrusts with movements of her own. She held on to his shoulders, sensed the slight desperation in his lovemaking, then held him closer. When she was in bed with Daniel, when they communicated with their bodies, she never wanted to let him go.

He drew out their lovemaking, rolling them over so she was on top of him. Cupping the back of her neck, pulling her down so he could kiss her. Then sliding away from her, deftly positioning her so he could enter from behind, holding her hips and thrusting strongly again.

But they finished face-to-face in an intimate embrace, Daniel on top of her, his weight resting on his elbows, her face cupped in his big hands, her legs wrapped around him. He watched her as she came again; and she felt his total focus on her and her pleasure. Then, and only then, did he allow himself his own release.

Daniel didn't let her go for long moments after he'd

finished. He kept her pinned to the bed, his sex still hard and full inside her. Gradually his arousal diminished, then he slid to the side, kissing her the entire time.

Meg didn't know why, but she felt like bursting into tears, like holding him close and never letting him go. Feeling too full of emotion and not wanting to say something she would regret, she kept her eyes closed.

She heard Daniel move around her hotel room, find his clothes and dress. He strode to the door, and even with her eyes closed and her face buried in the pillow, she felt his hesitation—that exquisite, painful moment when she sensed they both seemed poised to say something—

Then he opened the motel-room door, walked outside into the chill morning air and shut it. Meg lay quietly in the bed they'd just shared and felt as if one more thought about their relationship might send her over the edge.

But she was helpless to control those thoughts; she had to go there emotionally. Lying in the rumpled sheets, Meg envisioned Daniel returning to his ranch, alone. Eating breakfast by himself. Starting his endless round of chores. And for some reason that she wasn't ready to explain to herself, she burst into tears. Cried until she was spent. Then she curled up in the large, lonely bed that still smelled like him and finally slept.

But in that dark, subconscious moment before she drifted off, Meg wasn't at all sure she could leave Daniel again.

7

MEG WOKE UP WITH her neck still feeling a little sore, but a hot shower took most of the kinks out. Now, foremost in her mind was packing up, checking out of the motel, moving into one of Laura's guest rooms, and settling in for her extra week.

She'd already called home and talked with a friend who was house-sitting her apartment, watering her plants and feeding her two cats and Sluggo. Sluggo was getting on in years, and Meg didn't have the heart to board him out at the vet's. The little pug hated being confined in a kennel, and liked his routine just the way it was. If he slept in a patch of sunshine and quietly snored away most of the day, that was fine with him. And with Meg.

So the decks were cleared for another week in Blue Spruce, and the ten-year reunion was almost over. All she had to do was make it through the barbecue this afternoon, have that lunch with Susie sometime during the week and return the award, and then she could figure out the real question, the six-million-dollar question.

What was going to happen with Daniel?

She walked into the motel's tiny coffee shop, ordered coffee and buttered cinnamon-and-raisin toast to go, then returned to her room and commenced with her packing. That took all of ten minutes. Then, since it was only a little after eight, she took out her laptop computer and set it up. Turned it on. Stared at the color screen.

And wondered if she'd lost her nerve.

It took a peculiar kind of courage to keep sending novels out into the void, as she thought of it. That courage was all that kept her going, especially after her second and third novels were repeatedly rejected. The fourth—what she was working on now—was something much more commercial.

And she hated it.

You had the courage to write about Daniel's family. Too bad you can't say the same about your own.

Meg stared at the computer screen, wondering where that idea had come from.

It's true, the little voice nagged her.

And she knew she'd been given a gift. It had been part of the reason she'd come back to Blue Spruce. To get back to her roots—to that deep, creative part of herself; to the fearless girl she had lost somewhere along the way.

The idea tantalized her. Intrigued her. And scared her to death.

Oh, do it! She won't read it, anyway. She didn't read the first one, what makes you think she would make an exception for the second?

Meg turned off the computer and reached for her black leather carrying case. She found a yellow legal pad and a black pen, dug them out and threw them onto the large bed. She'd never been able to stand writing down ideas and playing with the structure of a novel on a computer.

But once she had her basic road map created, nothing stopped her.

Memories flooded her mind, thick and fast. Her mother had been fleeing a jealous ex-husband when they'd landed in Blue Spruce. It had been a place so unlike the usual locales Antonia had favored, it had taken Meg a while to understand why. Her mother had been in hiding, scared of that man's volatile temper. Afraid of his anger.

If Antonia Prescott had possessed one fatal flaw, it had been that she'd always looked to a man, and marriage, to rescue her from any unpleasantness in life. She'd never developed a skill or a talent to call her own, unless you could count the speed and efficiency with which she spent a current husband's money.

Thus, when she'd found another wealthy man willing to marry her and take her away to a life of relative ease, back in Manhattan, she hadn't wasted any time. Meg could still remember arriving home one day to find her mother perfectly dressed and coiffed, her suitcases in the foyer.

"You're eighteen now, and just about graduated," she'd said quickly as Meg had come in the door. Her mother had started, finished, and totally controlled that conversation. "There's no need for me to stay, what with Martin wanting me to join him back east. The rent's paid up until the end of the month, then you'll have to find another place to stay."

That had been it. Hello, Manhattan, and goodbye, motherhood. Antonia had left in a cloud of expensive scent, and Meg had watched from the front window as her mother had stepped into a taxi and out of her life.

She'd sat in the living room, numb. She'd raced home to tell her mother she was to give a special speech at the graduation ceremony. Not valedictorian, but second runner-up. Meg had been happy, until she'd seen those suitcases.

At dusk, she'd finally broken down and called Laura. Then she hadn't been able to do anything but cry. Laura had driven over in her old Chevy Impala, and told her that her grandmother had insisted Meg stay with them until she decided what to do.

What her mother had done had been one of the reasons she'd lit out for Los Angeles so soon after graduation. She'd sworn Laura to secrecy concerning it. And years passed before Meg herself had been able to face the implications of Antonia's actions.

So, she thought a little shakily, *do you have the guts to explore it in your writing?*

She uncapped one of the felt pens, stared at the yellow lined pad.

It's way past time, that little voice inside seemed to whisper, guiding her to her own true North, much like a needle on a compass. And Meg knew, with sudden clarity, that even if she never published what she was going to—what she *had* to—write, it was long past time to get it all down on paper. To remember, and finally put it to rest.

She took a sip of her coffee. A bite of toast. An excitement so strong it almost made her sick to her stomach started to well up deep inside. An excitement she hadn't felt in a long time.

Meg put pen to paper and began to write.

DANIEL FED THE DOGS and horses, then headed inside to fix himself some breakfast. He whipped up a bowl of oatmeal, with cinnamon and raisins. Coffee on the side, and if he was still hungry, he would fry up some eggs.

He wasn't. Breakfast just wasn't as much fun without Meg. Daniel wasn't sure he knew exactly why. He just knew he'd loved seeing her sitting at the breakfast bar, the sunlight caught in her hair. That infectious smile. Even the way she ate, digging into her food as if it were her last meal.

He ate quietly, finishing up the hot cereal. He gave the last few raisins to the ever-watchful Molly, then sat for a moment, thinking.

The barbecue was today. This afternoon, at the Community Center, by the pool. He and Meg hadn't talked about attending together, but he could call her and ask.

Then again, what was the point? He would simply be delaying the inevitable. She would be leaving shortly afterward, and he wondered if he should just let it go. She would probably call him before she left.

Great seeing you again, Daniel. We'll have to get together the next time I'm in town....

No, that didn't sound like Meg. But he knew she would be going back. He'd seen a different side of her last night, at dinner. Talking about a city she loved. The bookstores, the classes. The excitement and stimulation. The city that never slept.

In contrast, he was always up at dawn, and worked

so hard he was usually ready for bed by ten at the latest.

He'd played out so many scenarios in his head. Meg staying in Blue Spruce. The two of them getting married. But as the years passed, Daniel knew the one thing he couldn't bear would be if one day she looked at him and he saw regret in those blue eyes. Regret that she'd somehow shortchanged herself by staying with him.

Regret that she'd let him drag her down.

In another scenario, he went back to Los Angeles with her. And in short order, probably embarrassed her in front of her artistic, sophisticated friends. Meg was so quick, so vibrant, so electrically alive. So curious, and into everything. She reminded him of a little calico cat he'd had as a child—always playful, always loving; into everything and totally unrepentant when caught.

She was as unique, beautiful and delicate as a butterfly. And just as hard to catch.

He got up, walked to the sink and rinsed his dishes. As he looked out the large kitchen window over the sink, he saw Digger and Molly crouched down low by the garden fence, most likely awaiting the renegade rabbit who had been visiting the vegetable patch lately.

He felt a nudge against his leg, then glanced down at Hunter, looking up at him.

"Come," he said softly, and the shepherd mix fell into step behind him. Daniel took his mug of coffee out onto the front porch and sat down on the steps. Chores could wait for a few minutes.

"It's like this," he said, scratching the floppy, black-

and-tan ears. "I want her to stay, but I can't ask her. She has to want it."

He paused, looking at the gentle brown eyes. Hunter, just by being the dog she was, defined the word *compassion*.

"I know Meg, and she doesn't even know what she wants now. She's up in the air, and she doesn't need me making her decisions for her."

Hunter nudged his hand, gave his fingers a gentle lick.

"She worked so hard to get out of here." He continued to scratch the silky ears. "She found a place where she isn't different, after all."

Hunter sighed, then hunkered down on the porch, lying with her furry back pressed against his leg.

"I've loved her for so long...I don't even think I knew how much until I saw her that night at Duffy's. It all came back."

Hunter remained silent, gazing up at him. She'd shifted so her head rested on his jeans-clad thigh.

"Those two nights...they were a gift. I thought, afterward, that they would be enough. Would have to be enough. But I'm finding that...I want more, and I'm not sure it's right."

He reached down, stroked the dog's furry head. Took a sip of his coffee. It had cooled, but was still good.

"I want to talk about all this with her. That's one of the things I love about Meg. She's easy to be with." He laughed self-consciously then, and set his coffee down on the top porch step. "Unless I'm all tied up in knots."

He was silent for a time, finishing his coffee. He

gazed out at the mountains. There were so many memories for him on this land—both good and bad. His father and his mother. His brothers, and the time they'd spent growing up, coming of age on the ranch, learning from his father how to become men.

Then that horrible time right after his Daddy had been killed, when he'd walked out into one of the bare fields and stared up at the cold, gray winter sky, feeling totally shattered inside. And he'd realized, with a sort of numbing clarity, that he was now the oldest. The man of the family, with all the responsibilities that position entailed. And he'd known, even at that moment, that he could handle anything, could understand anything but his mother's relentless and all-consuming bitterness.

In time, after her death, he would come to understand even that.

He thought back to how he'd felt as each of his brothers had left. And when his mother had finally passed on. Then it had felt right to demolish the old ranch house and build something new. He'd wanted to fill this new house with good memories. Happy ones. Now, as he sat quietly on the porch, he realized just how solitary his life had become.

He had Meg to thank for that. She'd provided the contrast.

He continued to look at the mountains, and he thought about the long, cold winter that was coming, and how much more lonely this one would be. Because after loving Meg the way he had this summer, he would know what he was missing. Every single day.

"I should be like one of those guys in the movies. Just grab her and sweep her off her feet."

Hunter whined, then licked his hand again.

"Not a good idea, huh?"

She whined.

"Not my style, anyway."

Hunter remained silent.

"I could call her and pick her up for the barbecue."

Hunter's tail gently thumped against the porch floor.

"You like that idea?"

The tail thumped harder.

"I do, too." He finished his coffee, gave his dog one last pat, then got up and headed into the house.

SHE ARRIVED AT LAURA'S at eleven, with everything she'd brought with her in the trunk of her rental car.

"The last room on the right, all the way down," Laura said, reaching for one of her bags. "I changed the sheets this morning." She grabbed last night's award with her other hand.

"Are you going to the barbecue?" Meg asked.

"Wouldn't miss it! You know what happened last night? I got to talking to some of our old schoolmates, and a lot of other people are divorced. You wouldn't believe it—"

Meg listened as she and Laura carried her things upstairs to a beautiful bedroom, done in cheerful yellows with delicate cream walls. African violets perched on the windowsill, and the room was shaded by the enormous maple tree outside.

Meg sat on the comfortable bed, then touched a lacy

pillowcase. The border was a riot of embroidered roses, in varying shades of peach, pink and apricot.

"This is beautiful."

"Oh, I just do it in my spare time."

"No, I mean all of it." She got up off the bed, walked over to her friend, threw her arms around her and gave her an enormous hug.

"Meg." Laura seemed surprised as she hugged her back.

"Thank you," she said, then stepped away. "These last few days haven't been easy for me, and this room seems like a little sanctuary."

"That's exactly what it should be. Now, I don't want you thinking that you have to be down in the salon or entertaining anyone while you're here. There's a desk over there on that wall, you can set up your computer and work, or you can just sit downstairs on the porch and look out at the lake."

"Thank you."

Meg watched as Laura studied the bouquet of roses she'd brought over from the motel, then her friend gave her what she'd always referred to as "that look."

"You're not going to discuss Daniel with me, are you?"

"I...can't. I don't know what's going on."

Laura nodded her head. "*That* I understand. Well, here's a key. You don't have to report in to me if you get lucky with Daniel, you can eat anything you want in the refrigerator, and I want you to make yourself completely at home."

"Thank you, Laura."

"Hey, it's not L.A., but—"

"It's perfect."

SHE WORKED FOR ANOTHER hour, then showered and dressed for the barbecue. Jeans and a House of Blues T-shirt. Casual all the way.

The phone rang as she was running a comb through her hair, and she heard Laura answer it downstairs on her private line, not the salon's.

"Meg? She's right here. I hope you're coming to the barbecue, Daniel."

Meg came down the stairs and took the cordless phone, her heart pounding rapidly. She didn't know what to do. Playing it cool with a friend like Daniel didn't make sense. But they'd crossed that line two nights ago, and now she felt as if she were flying blind.

"Hi, Daniel."

"Hi." She heard him clear his throat over the line. "I didn't mean to call this late, but I had a little trouble tracking you down."

"I'm sorry. I should have left a message on your machine."

Silence. She regretted the words as soon as they were out of her mouth. Daniel didn't have an answering machine. He had no reason to use one.

"I should probably get one," he said.

"I shouldn't have said that," she said.

"Don't be so hard on yourself."

She didn't know what to say. Laura was watching her, a worried expression on her face.

"Can you hold on just a minute?" Meg asked, then started up the stairs. She had a few things she wanted to say to Daniel, and they had to be said in private.

"Sure."

Once she reached her bedroom and sat down in a chair overlooking the backyard and lake, she tried to gather her thoughts.

"Daniel, I'm sorry about last night."

"Don't be."

"No, I feel as if I forced you to stay with me—"

"Then why am I calling and asking you if you'd like some company at the barbecue?"

"And then what?" The words popped out of her mouth before she could stop them.

"Then...then, I guess you go back home."

There. He'd said it. Their lives would not converge. But he'd said it in such a quiet, honest way that she knew he wasn't playing a game with her. He just didn't want to hurt her. Her eyes stung and she bit her lip, then forced the next words out.

"What if I told you I wasn't going home right away?"

Silence. She could tell he needed a little time to digest this.

"How long are you going to stay?"

She heard it. The tiniest thread of hope in his voice. Her heart picked up speed.

"Another week or so. Whatever feels right."

"I'm glad."

"Okay." She took a deep breath, feeling as if she were on emotional overload. "Why don't we go to that barbecue?"

THE BLUE SPRUCE Community Center had been done up in purple and white—another huge banner welcoming back the high-school class. Long before Daniel and Meg found a parking place, they could smell what was in store for them.

Laura had insisted on driving her own car. Meg had offered her a ride, but her friend had given her another dose of "that look," then said under her breath, "I think the two of you need some time alone. And if I'm right, you won't be coming home tonight!"

Meg hadn't argued with her.

Once again, Susie had gone all out. The local Moose Lodge was in charge of the chicken on the grill, and Duffy had brought his famous spareribs and sauce. Susie had also made sure that Don's Drive-In, owned by a local man named Tony Morino, contributed several of their incredibly good briskets, along with both hot and sweet Italian sausages and French rolls for their world-class sandwiches.

Vats of barbecue sauce simmered beside the grilling meats. As Susie explained to them once she'd caught sight of Meg and rushed over, everyone could have their choice of chicken, ribs, brisket on a roll—or all three.

"You're going to make me gain weight!" Laura protested.

"Well, you could use some!" Susie roared with laughter. Sizing up both Laura and Meg, she said, "By our fifteen-year reunion, my one goal in life is to look like the two of you!" She hesitated. "I mean, like *one* of you. Unfortunately, right now I *do* look like the two of you!"

"Susie, you're not that heavy," Meg said.

"Honey, you're sweet, but I know there's plenty of

room for improvement! Laura, I'm coming to your salon next week. I think I made an appointment for this
Wednesday. I want you to do something with my
hair—the last guy just *ruined* it. And Meg, I have to
know your secret! I've watched you eat and eat like a
trucker all weekend, and you haven't gained an
ounce!"

"She burns it off thinking up all those racy plots,"
Kevin said, coming up behind his wife and putting an
arm around her. "I say today's a day to forget diets and
dig in!"

"I agree," Meg said. She was determined to have a
good time, to enjoy her classmates and the glorious
weather, the good food and camaraderie.

And Daniel, most of all. Whatever happened afterward, she wanted to be ready for it.

They moved along through the various booths,
sturdy paper plates in hand. The sheer amount of food
was staggering, the choices seemed limitless. First rel-
ish plates, followed by a wedge of iceberg lettuce with
Thousand Island dressing or a large spoonful of green-
bean casserole.

Then the meats: chicken, ribs, the infamous brisket
or Italian sausage.

Meg pondered her choice, knowing Daniel was
watching her, amused as always.

"I want brisket and sausage on the same roll, with
one rib on the side. And a drumstick. Oh, and the barbecue sauce on the side, too."

"*Where* does she put it?" Susie wailed.

Daniel only laughed.

"Susie," Heather said. "You've found your calling! I think you should open a restaurant!"

People laughed good-naturedly while Susie beamed.

Then came the side dishes. Meg paused, considering her choices. Baked beans, marinated mushrooms, macaroni and cheese, onion sour-cream pie and coleslaw. Roasted potatoes with various herb butters. And grilled French bread with garlic butter.

"She's stumped!" Kevin called out.

Meg simply smiled.

"Do you want me to go ahead?" Daniel asked.

"Nope. I know what I want." She smiled sweetly at the women behind the long counters. "Could I please have a separate plate and have a little serving of each? They all look so good, I want to try them all."

"She's going for the record!" another classmate yelled.

"You'd better eat it all or I'll have to spank you," Bruno said, coming up behind Meg and wiggling his eyebrows. Today he was dressed the same as he'd been at Duffy's on Friday night, in faded jeans and a Harley-Davidson T-shirt.

The look Daniel gave him spoke volumes, and Laura started to laugh.

Susie bustled up to join them.

"Now, save some room for the baked goods we have for dessert! And homemade ice cream, too! There's cold lemonade at the tables already, and I thought we could all sit over there." She indicated a whitewashed picnic table, one of many beneath a large, striped tent.

Meg looked up at Daniel and he shrugged his shoulders as if to say, "It's your decision."

"Fine with me," she said to Susie.

"That's great, because a couple of the girls have your book with them, and they wanted to know if you—if you could—if you weren't too busy—"

"Of course I'll sign them."

HE'D NEVER BEEN surrounded by more food in his life.

Or felt less like eating.

Meg staying in Blue Spruce another week? Another seven days? He'd thought she was heading out of town that evening. Or at the latest, the following morning.

How on earth was he supposed to keep from thinking about her for another week? Or keep his hands off her?

He pushed his food around on his plate as he pretended to eat, and watched her. With two plates in front of her, along with a giant glass of homemade lemonade, she made a valiant attempt to dig into the huge lunch. But once again, classmates kept stopping by, this time with copies of her novel, both hardback and paperback.

She took time with each person, trying to make the autograph more than simply "Best Wishes" or "Happy Reading." And Daniel knew those books would go home to places of honor on bookshelves, on mantels, even in china cabinets and hutches. Because in Blue Spruce, it wasn't every day someone met a real live author.

"Hey, let her eat!" Bruno said almost twenty

minutes later, and Daniel immediately wished he'd been the man who had voiced that sentiment.

"Yeah, I want to see if she can pack it all away," someone else called out.

"Do I hear a dare?" Meg said, and a few people laughed. She picked up her fork and dug into the baked beans.

Fifteen minutes later, Daniel had no idea how a woman Meg's size could put away that much food.

"This is fabulous," Meg said, as Susie looked on, smiling. "I haven't had barbecue this good in ages."

"What about at The House of Blues?" Bruno asked, referring to her T-shirt.

"Nope," Meg said around a mouthful of sausage and brisket sandwich.

The afternoon passed lazily, with laughter and reminiscing. Meg signed a few more books. Several of the women who wanted signed copies also had their children with them, as this was the most casual day of the reunion. A day for families.

Daniel didn't miss the expression in Meg's eyes as she held one particularly sweet baby. And he wondered if she'd ever thought about having children. She would make a wonderful mother, he knew that much. Meg had so much empathy, and such a sense of fun. She also knew what it was like to grow up with a mother who hadn't really cared, so he felt sure she would put all the time and care she had into raising any children she chose to have.

The thought brought a queer little ache to his chest.

It also made him think about the three times they'd made love, and the fact that he hadn't even considered using protection with her. And hadn't bothered to ask her if she was using anything.

Not very responsible; but everything had been different with Meg. Every emotion he'd ever felt while making love had been intensified. He couldn't honestly say he'd ever loved any woman besides Meg, and what he'd found while making love to her was that *love* made all the difference.

He watched her, content to sit slightly on the sidelines and make sure she had her day. He noticed that she did a very subtle job of bringing her classmates out of themselves, making sure they told her all about their lives. She was genuinely interested in what they had to say, and he realized all over again just how much he cared for her.

THE SUN SANK LOWER in the sky. Dessert was served. Grown-up banana splits with homemade ice cream in five different flavors—chocolate, vanilla and strawberry, along with fresh peach and peppermint. Several gourmet sauces, along with bowls of sliced bananas, shredded coconut and cashews were available to spoon over the cool dessert.

And homemade cookies—chocolate chip, peanut butter, and oatmeal. Susie had gone easy on the cakes, as last night had put everyone into cake overload. But summer in Blue Spruce meant fresh-baked berry pies, and the tables were loaded with five different varieties.

The air grew cooler, as a breeze from the mountains picked up. Meg and Daniel, along with a group of classmates, moved from the picnic tables to the deck chairs beside the large community pool, where they lounged and continued talking. No one wanted the barbecue to end. After this Sunday, people had planes to catch and jobs to go back to on Monday and Tuesday. Real life would intervene, and this ten-year reunion, this weekend out of time, would become a happy memory.

Babies and toddlers started to fuss, and mothers and fathers began to pack up. Daniel and Bruno had gone over and offered their services to the men from the Moose Lodge, and were now helping to fold up chairs and carry tables inside.

Older children played on the lawn that sloped down to the Community Center. Meg watched as a boy she knew from her junior-year English class, now a father of two, ended a dispute between his two young sons and herded them off toward the family car.

All in all, a peaceful and successful day.

If she were honest with herself, she was glad the reunion was over. Now, with seven more days in Blue Spruce, she had a chance to see what would happen between her and Daniel.

She wouldn't use lovemaking to push the issue. She wouldn't push him, period. The strange thing was, she knew he wanted to be with her, yet she sensed a certain reluctance on his part. And she didn't know what that was about.

Her eyes drifted shut. Stuffed with good food, exhausted from the nonstop activity of the three-day reunion, she'd almost drifted into a light doze when an unpleasantly familiar voice jolted her awake.

"Well, if it isn't Little Miss Filthy Rich herself."

She opened one eye and looked up.

Paula. And she was not happy.

8

MEG EYED HER adversary cautiously from her reclining position on a chaise longue by the pool.

Paula had the flushed face and reddish eyes of someone who had been drinking too much. Although only ice-cold beer had been available at the barbecue, that hadn't prevented anyone from bringing their own liquid refreshment.

As Meg studied Paula's face, she noticed the puffiness around her jawline, the dark circles beneath her eyes, and the pronounced creases that ran from her nose to the corners of her thin, downturned mouth.

Paula had not aged well. Nonstop drinking and smoking hadn't helped. Nor had the negative thoughts that now seemed etched into her expression. She'd always been one of the meanest kids in class, and had grown into a vindictive woman. And she obviously blamed the world for the way her life had turned out, not stopping to think that she might have had a single thing to do with it.

"Aren't you going to say anything?" Paula demanded, hands on hips, glaring down at her.

"Nope." Meg decided to make it really clear from the start that she wasn't going to rise to any baiting from this woman. She didn't want a fight. Not now, and not with Paula.

"Well, I wanna know something."

"Paula, please—" Susie began.

Paula glared at her. "Pipe down." The woozy woman turned her attention back to Meg. "I wanna know who the hell you think you are, waltzing into town like you own the place, thinking you can come back here when you were never a part of—"

"Paula, that's enough!" Now Susie was clearly upset, and Meg realized she had to do something. The class reunion had been spectacularly well put together, and she knew the entire class had Susie to thank for that. She couldn't bear to sit by and let the woman be hurt.

And she didn't want everyone remembering the end of the reunion this way.

"Paula."

That got the woman's attention. She turned her head again and focused in on Meg.

"Your beef's with me. Not her." Meg got up from the chaise, willing her legs to remain steady. Willing her breathing to stay calm and deep. She wouldn't let this woman mess with her mind.

"You got that right!"

"Okay, then. Let's take it over there." Meg indicated the other end of the pool with a nod. "There's no reason to spoil everyone's good time."

Meg knew it was completely bizarre that Paula agreed with her, but the thought ran through her head that the woman probably wanted to give her a thorough trouncing, so any way she could get her to rise to a fight, she would take.

"You got it."

"Fine." Thinking quickly, Meg walked toward the far end of the pool, keeping an eye on Paula.

"UH-OH, I SEE trouble," Bruno said, shading his eyes and squinting. "Paula's got Meg."

"*What?*" Daniel set down the folding chair he'd been carrying, and started toward the pool area at a dead run.

"I DON'T WANT TO FIGHT with you, Paula," Meg said clearly, slowly. She wanted to make sure the inebriated woman understood.

"I don't want to fight with you, Paula," she mimicked right back, making Meg's words sound as if they were full of fear.

Meg simply ignored her and continued.

"So that's why I'm giving you this chance to turn around and walk away. No one will think any less of you. In fact, I think they'd admire you for choosing to walk away from a fight."

"You and your fancy words." Paula smiled, but it didn't reach her bloodshot eyes. "I'm gonna enjoy beating on you."

Meg watched as the woman moved in, then raised her hands in a defensive stance.

DANIEL WAS ALMOST there when it happened.

Everyone in Blue Spruce would talk about it for years to come. One minute, Paula rushed Meg like an enraged rhino. The next, Meg stepped aside, placed a well-aimed chop and a kick, then flipped her into the deep end of the pool with an enormous splash.

No one moved. No one said a word as Paula surfaced in the rippling, turquoise water, sputtering and swearing, then screaming as she paddled furiously to stay afloat. It took a few seconds for anyone to think about jumping in and saving her, then one of the volunteer firemen got the thankless job.

Daniel reached Meg's side a heartbeat later.

"Meg!" He grabbed her, pulling her into his arms. She was shaking, and buried her head against his chest.

"I didn't start anything—" she began.

Crazily enough, he thought of her mother, remembering that time in the principal's office when he and Meg first met.

"I know you didn't, Blue."

"She's just—obsessed with me." Meg lifted her head and watched, and he followed her gaze to where two volunteer firemen and Steve Batten, the local sheriff, were trying to restrain Paula. The woman was still struggling, shooting venomous glances at Meg. Even Daniel could feel the hatred in her eyes.

"I think it's time to leave," he said.

"I think *she* should leave," Meg said.

He held Meg until she stopped shaking, and they both watched as Steve walked a soaking-wet Paula to his patrol car. Then, as she began to mouth off, cursing and resisting being restrained, he cuffed her and tucked her into his back seat. Turning on the flashing red lights, Steve drove the police car out the huge circular drive of the Community Center and headed south, toward the station in town.

"A fitting tribute and ending to a wonderful day,"

Kevin quipped from behind them. "I always knew this class was unique."

"I'm sorry," Meg said as she turned toward him.

"For what? She was the problem."

"How'd you do that?" Someone small had bumped into Meg and was now tugging at the hem of her T-shirt. Daniel watched as Meg glanced down. A small towheaded boy looked up at her, his freckled face wearing an expression of genuine admiration.

"Do what?"

"Flip her like that. You're a *girl*, and she was *way* bigger!"

"I took some karate classes."

He considered this. "Cool. Like Batman."

Daniel watched as Meg's mouth twitched. He knew she wanted to smile. He certainly did.

"No. Like *Cat*woman."

"Yeah! That was *neat!*"

"Brian, you get over here!" a mother yelled.

"I still think it was cool," he muttered, before darting away.

"Setting a fine example for the young ones, are we?" Bruno said as he walked up.

Daniel knew the exact moment she started to lose it. The look in her eyes. The way she bit her lip, gripped his hand. He didn't waste any time.

"I think we'll head out."

What he did next he knew would be talked about at least as long as Paula's quick trip into the pool, but he was beyond caring. All he was concerned about was Meg.

He picked her up, one arm around her shoulders, the

other beneath her bent knees, and carried her down the grassy hill, past the Community Center, out into the parking lot and straight to his pickup.

SHE DIDN'T SAY A WORD until they were almost halfway to his ranch.

"I guess I do."

Her voice was so soft he almost didn't hear her.

"Do what?"

"Make a habit of this." And with that, she started to cry.

He pulled the truck over onto the shoulder and took her into his arms.

"Oh, baby, don't. Don't do this to yourself."

He let her cry it out. Ached for her. Gave her his handkerchief, then started the pickup and headed the rest of the way to his ranch.

"What are we doing here?" she said as he killed the ignition.

"I thought you might—"

"You thought I might get into more trouble if you didn't keep an eye on me."

He took a deep breath. She still had to be upset and angry about what Paula had pulled on her. Even scared. And she was inadvertently taking it out on him, because he was there, and a safe target for her frustration. Well, he would help her ride out this upsetting night.

"No, that's not what I meant. I thought you might want to get away from everything for a while. And relax."

She closed her eyes, and he could almost feel the

struggle going on inside. After almost a full minute, she spoke.

"Okay. Maybe a cup of coffee. And maybe a little something else one of the women in town baked for you."

His mouth twitched. He couldn't help it. It wasn't in Meg's nature to be petty, but she'd found out a couple of things at the barbecue over the desserts.

Betty Sue might be married, but he received a regular stream of cookies, cakes and pies from several of the single ladies in Blue Spruce. It was the damnedest thing, as if they were auditioning or something.

"All right," he said.

"And then I'm going home."

"Whatever you want, Blue."

"Right after coffee. Just coffee."

"Your call."

"Thanks. Okay. I'm ready."

And with that, she got out of the truck and marched toward the front porch. He followed right behind, taking the opportunity to admire her in those tight, faded jeans. And he suddenly realized he'd never liked a fiery temper in a woman until she'd shown him hers.

THEY NEVER DRANK that coffee.

She was still angry as they entered the ranch house, and he could almost feel her temper as she turned toward him.

"Daniel, I just don't get it."

"What?" He'd gone to the kitchen and was giving the dogs some dry food as they pranced around him, whining and begging for their dinner.

"Why don't you want to go to bed with me?"

He threw the plastic scoop back inside the forty-pound bag of kibble and closed the pantry door.

And stared at her.

She didn't back down.

"Well?" she said, and crossed her arms over her chest. Stuck out her chin. "What's wrong with me? Why don't you want me?"

He took a deep breath. "You've got it all wrong, Blue. I've wanted you since I was sixteen years old. The thoughts I had about you could have landed me in jail."

She looked as if he'd just sucker punched her.

He felt as if he'd opened a box he'd kept locked for far too long. He'd been sitting on the lid, trying to keep everything inside, and now that he'd started, he couldn't stop.

"I was jealous of my own brother all those years ago, because he had the guts to ask you out when I didn't. I didn't think I had anything to offer a girl like you, anyway. All my time was taken up with responsibilities at home."

She just stared, but he could see the shock in her eyes, the deep realization. Maybe it was better this way. Maybe he would just tell her, all at once, how he'd always felt about her. Maybe he would scare her off, and settle this whole issue once and for all. She would probably ask him to drive her back to Laura's house tonight, then she would change her flight and head out to Los Angeles as soon as she could.

"You think those two nights we had together are all I want? Hell, Blue, I've dreamed about you since the day you left. In my bed, in the barn, in the shower, on the floor—" He took another breath, and felt as if he were fighting for air.

"None of those damn dreams came anywhere close to what we shared. If I had my way, I'd keep you locked up in my bedroom and make love to you every night so you wouldn't even be able to stand up the next morning."

He took a deep breath, shaking from the strength of his emotions. Then he saw that she was smiling. *Smiling!* It lit his temper and he took a few steps toward her.

"Get out of the house and go sit in the truck."

"No."

"*Now.*"

She didn't move.

"Don't stay here, Blue, 'cause you know what's going to happen if you do."

She nodded her head, and he noticed her hand was at her throat, where her pulse beat strongly. Her eyes were steady as she looked at him, the room quiet except for the ticking of the kitchen clock and the sound of three hungry dogs crunching their dry food.

He stood there, struggling for control, knowing in his heart he was fighting a losing battle. He closed his eyes and willed himself to have the strength to walk away from her. Because if he made love to her again, he wasn't sure he would be able to let her go. And he didn't want to think about being reduced to begging her to stay.

"Please," he whispered. That one painful word was as close to begging as he ever wanted to get.

"I can't…. I need you, Daniel."

Those words shocked him so much he opened his eyes, looked directly at her.

"I need you so much, I'm shaking with it."

He saw the truth in her eyes. And gave in.

He started toward her.

SHE'D FINALLY UNLEASHED a part of him she'd always known was there. And she'd done it with deliberate intent.

Daniel was her friend, had been one of her oldest and best friends. So why did she feel that sudden frisson of fear as he came toward her?

More like a thrill, that she could do this to him. Reduce him to a male animal, totally out of control.

Then she stopped thinking as he swept her up into his arms, over his shoulder, and started down the long hallway. They made it to the bedroom, where he threw her down across his big bed and swiftly stripped off her shoes, her T-shirt, then her jeans and panties.

Meg didn't say a word, her heart thundering in her chest. She couldn't. All she could do was close her eyes and lie back as sensation after sensation imprinted on her. The feel of his large hands as she arched her hips and let him pull her jeans down and off. The roughness of his palms as his fingers slipped beneath the elastic of her pink panties. The cool air on her naked skin.

The sound of his boots hitting the carpet, the rustle of jeans coming off. She opened her eyes a mere slit, in time to see his T-shirt being whipped up and off his powerfully muscled chest, then sailing through the air to land with their other clothing on the floor.

Then he was up and over her. Inside her. No more warning than that. Foreplay at this point would have been ridiculous, as she was ready for him, accepted him, tilted her pelvis to take more of him, grabbed at his back, his buttocks. She closed her eyes again, hearing his low groan, feeling his weight on top of her—the hard, ridged muscles of his abdomen, the crisp chest hair.

Then she could no longer define the sensations as all her feelings went into overdrive.

Fast, furious, needing each other so badly there were no words, he slammed into her repeatedly and she reached completion as swiftly as he did. His climax came right on top of hers; she could barely hear his sharp moans through her own peculiar haze of satisfaction. He buried his face in the side of her neck and made a sound so agonized she would have thought he was being tortured.

Then all was silent.

WHEN SHE AWOKE, she'd found he'd tucked her into his big bed lying in the right direction and was beside her, fast asleep. Night had fallen and claimed the land outside; no illumination relieved the darkness. Daniel slept on, breathing deeply, and she luxuriated in the feel of his arms, roped with muscles, wrapped tightly around her, as if even in sleep, he feared she would steal out the door and leave him.

She lay there, silent, wondering what was going to happen to them. And the only thing Meg was certain of was that they couldn't go on as before, living thousands of miles apart. They belonged together, and the sooner Daniel understood that fact, the better it would be for both of them.

She had no illusions that she would even come close to fitting the image of a typical rancher's wife. She hoped she wouldn't embarrass Daniel too much. Most of what she would need to do, he could teach her. She found herself wanting to help him in any way she could, wanting to ease the burden of his running this ranch all by himself.

She wanted to be a source of comfort to him.

I need you, Daniel.

He needed her, as well.

But she didn't believe Daniel had ever looked at ranching as a burden. The desire to do this sort of work was in his soul. He took after his father in that respect. Daniel loved the land, the animals he cared for. He loved growing things, seeing what he planted coming to fruition. Working outside, in the fresh air. She couldn't imagine him behind a desk, in an office.

He was a lot like Bob Willett—a patient, understanding man who knew how to be with people.

And he was more than enough for her. He always had been.

She thought of the copy of her novel on his bookshelf, and of all the ways she'd considered signing that title page. Now, only one came to mind.

To Daniel. I have loved you all my life....

He stirred, and she lost her train of thought as one callused hand moved up to her breast. Cupped the underside. Slid up over the nipple.

She held her breath.

He squeezed. Sighed. Murmured something.

She smiled. Daniel was still asleep.

So Meg lay quietly, her mind racing. All she could think of was how much she would miss this if she left. This man, this relationship. His arms around her, his hand on her breast, the way he looked at her when he thought she didn't notice. The way his deep gray eyes would light with pleasure when she entered a room.

He'd always been a rather serious boy, and a quiet man. She loved to make him laugh, to bring that particular joy into his eyes, his smile. He could look at her a certain way and simply take her breath away. And she was almost dead certain he had no idea what he did to her.

Meg took a long, slow breath, then snuggled closer to Daniel in the warm bed. She knew him in a deep way, as he did her. They'd grown up together, seen each other through some incredibly tough times. He was one of her oldest, dearest friends, because she and her mother had never stayed in one place for as long as they had in Blue Spruce.

Those high-school years she'd lived in the small town had given Meg a chance to finally put down some roots, even if there had been many moments when she'd felt she didn't belong—and never would.

Yet Meg knew that despite all the time she'd spent in Blue Spruce, neither she nor Daniel had been able to get past a certain point in their relationship. Until now. Now, things had finally changed. There would be no running away from this night, from this moment.

She'd come back for this. She knew that now. It hadn't been as much about finding herself creatively as it had been about finding Daniel. If nothing had happened between them, maybe she would have been able to accept it, go back to Los Angeles and decide to find a man out there.

She'd faced a deep truth in the past year, months before the reunion. She was tired of living alone in her one-bedroom apartment. Tired of eating her meals alone, facing an uncertain future alone. She'd discovered she wanted a partner in life, someone special to share things with. But every time the crucial question "Who?" had come up, every time that lonely little ache had throbbed in her chest, she'd seen Daniel in her mind's eye.

She'd also known what that decision would entail. Leaving her city—the bookstores and nightlife, the classes—and coming back to Blue Spruce. To this starkly beautiful land that held such a large piece of his heart. Well, she could cope. Books and research materials could be shipped. The Internet was at her fingertips. Things were a lot different ten years later. The world was smaller.

She was tough; she could cope. She wanted to cope, because she wanted to stay with Daniel.

Her only secret fear was that she couldn't bear for him to be laughed at if he chose to have a relationship with her. He was a man who was tightly woven into the fabric of Blue Spruce and its townspeople. Bob Willett had been loved and respected by everyone; his family had lived in the area forever.

In complete contrast, she and her mother had blown into town a scant fourteen years ago. And you didn't really belong in a small town like this one until you'd lived here for several generations; really dug your roots in.

Also, she was sure no one in town had forgotten the scathing remarks her mother had made the first few years they'd lived here. Small towns had long memories, with crystal-clear powers of retention. No one had liked Antonia Prescott's attitude, least of all Meg. But she knew she'd been tarred with the same brush. "City folk don't belong here," the townspeople's looks had said often enough, when she'd gone shopping with her mother.

Antonia's haughtiness hadn't refuted that opinion.

More than anything, Meg didn't want to embarrass Daniel. If this were a perfect world, he would have married a woman like Betty Sue years ago, and had four or five children by now. But he hadn't.

Meg knew she didn't have a whole lot of illusions left after working and living in Los Angeles. After coming face-to-face with what a career in the publishing business entailed. She saw the world clearly, and she knew what most of the people in Blue Spruce thought of her.

They saw her as a wild little chatterbox with the most bizarre ideas spouting out of her mouth. As a strange young girl who hadn't been content to merely settle down. What Meg had never been able to understand was how anyone could think her wants and needs were any different from any other person's.

Under the skin, we're all the same. The same fears, the same feelings, the same joys. She thought about this for a while in the dark, deeply enjoying the feel of Daniel's arms around her, holding her tight. And she knew then, that this was what she'd been trying to put across in her first novel: that no matter how strange our actions might look to others, in the end, we all really wanted the same things.

That peculiar creative electricity crackled in her mind, and she eased Daniel's arms away, slipped from the bed. Totally uncaring that she was naked, she reached for the pad of paper and pencil on the nightstand, then turned the bedside lamp to its lowest setting and began to write.

HE AWOKE SLOWLY, reaching consciousness to the sound of something scratching. He couldn't quite place it, and stretched, came further awake, opened his eyes.

Meg. Naked. Writing. Totally enthralled by what she was doing. For long moments, he simply enjoyed watching her from the depths of the bed, until she glanced up and saw that he was awake.

"Hi." The pencil wavered. Stopped.

"Go on," he said, his voice soft. "Keep writing."

The pencil hit paper again. "I'll only be a minute."

"Take as long as you want. There's a computer in the den if you need it."

"No, just some ideas that came into my head—"

He lay back, watching her write, and knew in his heart that Meg would never be a normal person. And thank God for that. He loved her exactly as she was; every single bit that made her such a unique woman.

She filled up one more page on the small, lined pad before she stopped, put the pencil down, and slid back between the sheets. He found he loved looking at the line of her back, the delicate and vulnerable curve of her neck. But he reached over and turned off the light.

She snuggled into his arms and he held her. Content.

"What was that? If you don't mind my asking."

"More ideas. Kind of a realization."

"Oh. For the new book."

"Uh-huh. I just kind of figured out what it was about. The first one, too."

"Just now?"

"Yeah. Sometimes it works that way."

He kissed her forehead, wondering at her mind and the things it could think up. Admiring her.

"Tired?" he asked.

"Not that tired."

He could hear her smile in the darkness, knew what she was really telling him.

He hesitated. "Did I hurt you, Meg?"

"No. I liked it." She kissed his neck. "I liked seeing that wild-man side. I hope to see it more often."

He hesitated.

"Are you okay?" she whispered.

He wanted to tell her all his fears. How much he loved her, and always would. How much he wanted her. Yet a part of him felt ashamed, as if to reveal so much, and such deep thoughts, would somehow be wrong. He couldn't hold her here that way.

And not for the first time, Daniel wished he'd grown up with a sister or two. A softer, feminine influence. He and his brothers had joked and laughed; there'd been lots of horseplay and energy. His mother had relegated herself to the sidelines emotionally, coming out only when she had to. His father had navigated his wife's difficult emotional waters; somehow Bob Willett had possessed that phenomenal ability to say the right thing at the right time.

Daniel felt all tied up in knots. The only thing he was sure of right now was how he felt about Meg. But he didn't know if he could say it.

"Daniel?" she whispered, and he could hear the aching vulnerability in her voice.

In answer, he pulled her even closer, found her mouth in the darkness, kissed her. Gently. He didn't know where that kiss would take them, but he knew he wanted to be close.

She sighed. Melted against him. Surrendered. He gathered her closer, deepened the kiss. Rose up over her, gathered her beneath him, took his weight on his forearms so he wouldn't squeeze the breath out of her.

Kissed her again. And again. Her forehead, her cheekbones, her neck. Then her mouth. And he felt that pulse-pounding excitement that only this woman made him feel. That, and something so much more.

The feeling rose up inside him, and he knew he had to give it a voice. Had to say it. Finally.

"Meg," he whispered against her hair. "I love you."

9

HE FELT HER ANSWER in the exquisite tightening of her muscles. Her slightly indrawn breath. She moved even closer toward him, and he framed her face with his hands, tangling his fingers in her hair as he kissed her again. Deeply. Slowly. He didn't want this moment in time to ever end.

Something had finally been released inside him. Even if she left, she would know how he felt about her. He'd wanted to say it for years, and now he'd finally found the strength to express what he'd kept inside for so long.

Excitement caught. Held. Her hips pressed up against his as he took her mouth again. And again. He didn't care if she didn't say anything back. His declaration of love hadn't been made to wring the same confession out of her. He'd simply needed to say it, after all their time apart.

He'd already expressed his feelings for her through the sensual night rhythms of their lovemaking. Now he'd expressed them in words. And he would make the significance of what he said felt by the way he touched her. Before, when he'd flung her across the bed and stripped her clothing off, their coupling had been frantic. Frenzied. Furiously erotic. But here in his bed, deep in the heart of the night, he would take his time with her. He wanted, in the most primitive sense, to mark her. Make her his. Seek out every part of her body and touch it, taste it, kiss it.

He moved down her body slowly, and even when she caught and held his head, even when he heard her breathless sigh, he continued. Relentlessly. To her breasts, their softness and warmth, their exquisite sensitivity. Her small sighs and quick little groans excited him further, as he lavished each nipple with attention. He kissed the soft, warm undersides, then moved a little lower, to her rib cage.

She moaned softly in the dark bedroom, her hands catching his hair. Her fingers dug into his scalp in a way that told him the sensation was so acute she wanted him to stop. But he wouldn't. Couldn't. How had he ever thought that finally making love to Meg would drive her out of his system? If anything, it made him want her more. He didn't think there would ever be a time when he would tire of her.

He moved lower, kissing, caressing. Touching. Holding her firmly, his hands grasping her hips. Moving lower still to that feminine heart, that heat and scent and liquid warmth that promised him so much pleasure. She didn't play coy with him, didn't hesitate. At his gentle insistence, her thighs parted. He settled himself right where he wanted to be and pleasured her.

Now the rhythm quickened. He sensed she couldn't endure, didn't want to endure this type of lovemaking much longer. And he didn't want to wait. He wanted to be close to her, inside her. He wanted her happy.

Fulfilled. Content. He wanted that closeness, that claiming.

He slid up to her side, then grasped her hips and rolled them both over so she was straddling him. Threading his fingers through her hair, he eased her down, took her mouth. At the same time, he adjusted himself beneath her, guided his arousal toward the heart of her. He heard her sudden intake of breath, felt it against his mouth as he pushed inside—one smooth thrust that brought him a pleasure so intense he had to break their kiss for an instant.

She fell forward, her breasts hot against his chest, her breath soft on his face. Her arms came up around his neck, and he kissed her. She kissed him back, and he gave her time, built her arousal again, slowly, with lips and tongue. He didn't move his body at all until she rose up, straddling him, and began to thrust against him.

Those sensual, rocking movements could bring him to his knees. He felt the sound rise up out of his chest, then bit his lip against the low moan, concentrating on her pleasure, concentrating on *being* with her, feeling with her. Thrusting, pushing, establishing that other rhythm; that relentless, sensual slide.

His hands smoothed lower, over that soft skin, over her waist and down her hips. Cupping her bottom. Pulling her up close. Thrusting up at the same time and listening to her sharp cries.

Almost there... Almost...

He loved the moment when she shattered in his arms, the way she lost all control. Those exquisitely strong, feminine contractions took him over the edge and he thrust harder. More urgently. He held her even tighter then, clutching her hips as he pushed up, head back, eyes closed. And gave her everything, because he never wanted to be with anyone else, ever. She was his. He would find a way to keep her. He would never let her go.

The aftermath—as she slid down his body, gasping for breath, her chest heaving, her heart pounding—was gratifying for him. He was barely aware of his surroundings, his own release had been so intense. But he pulled her close, keeping her leg and arm draped over him as he closed his eyes and tried to slow his rapid breathing.

Minutes passed. Then, as consciousness slowly returned, he felt a warm dampness on his shoulder and realized she was crying.

Knowing, in that deepest part of himself, that this was not a time for words, he simply gathered her close in his arms and held her. Let her cry. Her release had been more than physical; walls had been breached. They'd talked around those walls for far too long. Words weren't necessary right now. He held her tightly against his chest as he kissed her, smoothed her hair off her wet face, kissed her again, and then kept her in his embrace until she fell asleep.

He turned toward her in the warm bed and slowly let exhaustion claim him, feeling more at peace with himself than he ever had been.

At peace because she was finally his. And always had been.

SHE DIDN'T LEAVE HIS ranch for two days.

He assumed she'd called Laura. They didn't drive

back to town to her house to pick up Meg's clothes because what he had planned for her didn't require any. He wanted her in his bed at all times, with short breaks while he saw to the ranch animals—his horses and dogs, the two goats and several chickens.

Back inside his home, Meg surrendered. And he finally sated a hunger that had been building for years. A hunger that surprised him with its intensity and that he hoped wouldn't overwhelm or frighten her.

But Meg, in her own way, was as earthy as he was. She welcomed him with a lusty abandon, and they made love throughout those forty-eight hours as if they'd just invented it.

There were so many different moods with her. Funny and teasing, with that beautiful smile and belly laugh. Strong and intense when he pinned her down, making her scream. And afterward, lying in each other's arms, dazed. Long and leisurely, making her beg for satisfaction, getting her so ready she fairly quivered with the need to finish, to find that sensual completion.

And the talking. Meg was a talker, and he found himself astounded when she told him how beautiful he was to her. When she took that most vulnerable part of him in her hands and admired it. He was humbled by her sensual honesty, even as he knew he would never be able to find the words to tell her how exquisite she was to him.

She was the one who dealt in words, who made language sing. She was the one who made verbal images come to life. He was a simpler man, who had to touch, to feel, to cup her breasts in his hands or smooth his palms down her back and hear that small sigh of feminine pleasure.

He loved her the best way he knew how, keeping her in his bed, bringing her food and feeding her. Letting her sleep when he sensed exhaustion was close. Holding her and watching her. Filling his senses with this woman he loved; this extraordinary, high-strung, brilliant butterfly of a girl.

"What are you thinking?" she'd asked him once, as he'd stretched out in his large bed and watched her. She'd been eating a peach, and he'd pulled her down across his chest and kissed the sweet juice off her lower lip, licked it from her chin. As unselfconscious as a child, she'd offered him a bite of the ripe fruit, then laughed at the expression on his face.

He hadn't wanted the peach; he'd wanted her.

He'd mock-wrestled the fruit out of her hands as she'd shrieked, then pinned her down on the bed, her hands above her head.

"How happy I am," he'd whispered against her hair, then eased up so he could see her face. It had fairly glowed with happiness.

"Me, too." She'd raised her head and kissed the tip of his nose. "But I want the rest of that peach."

"Hmm." He'd gazed down at her, delighting in teasing her. Making her smile. Just that smile would be enough, coming home to it every night. More than enough.

"The peach," she'd whispered, biting his earlobe.

"What do I get in return?"

"What do you *not* get?"

She'd looked so indignant he'd started to laugh, then

both of them had dissolved into fits of laughter when they'd seen Molly stealthily finishing off the remainder of the ripe fruit, which had fallen off the bed.

He'd left his bedroom, brought back two more peaches from the bowl on the kitchen counter, sliced them with a knife and hand-fed her the fragrant pieces. She'd watched him from her place on the bed, lying back against several pillows. And he'd known he would keep that image of her, naked and glowing, in his mind's eye for the rest of his life.

"I WANT TO SHOW YOU the stars," he said, late one night.

"You do?" she mumbled, a satiated tangle of arms and legs beneath the tumble of blankets.

He laughed, then got out of bed and reached for his jeans. Then he handed her his bathrobe.

"You're serious," she said, wrapping the large blue terry-cloth garment around her body.

"You'll like it," he said. "I have a telescope set up on the back porch. And it's a clear night." He checked the weather every day from habit, a habit so powerfully ingrained he rarely thought about it. His father had done it before him, and he would do it every day for the rest of his life. Now, this evening, he knew the night sky would be clear, affording them an excellent view of the heavens.

They traipsed outside toward the back porch. And he was pleasantly gratified when she gasped at the sight of the large telescope.

"Can we look at the moon?" she whispered.

"Sure. Anything you want." He looked through the

eyepiece, adjusted the telescope. "But why are you whispering?"

"I don't know. I guess looking up at that sky. It's so...immense."

"I know." He stepped back, then gestured for her to take a turn looking through the instrument. "It always puts my entire life back into perspective, whenever I look up into the sky. Especially the stars."

She stepped up to the telescope, her bare feet curling against the wooden porch floor. Rolling back the sleeves of the terry-cloth robe, she looked into the eyepiece.

"My God," she whispered.

He smiled. He'd placed the telescope so she would see a star, blazing away in the sky. They looked extraordinary through that powerful lens, like blazing balls of colored fire.

"It's gorgeous."

He stood silently beside her, waiting. Letting her look her fill. And wishing he could give her all the stars in the sky. All he had to offer her was himself and the ranch he'd built, and he was beginning to hope that it might just be enough.

"Don't you want to look?"

"Sure."

He took a turn, then focused the powerful instrument on the moon. A three-quarter moon, it glowed in the night sky among the twinkling stars. There was no sky on earth, Daniel decided at that moment, like a Colorado sky. Like seeing the stars against the backdrop of the Rockies.

"Take a look," he said, stepping back.

She did. She kept looking. They talked and observed the sky, switching angles. He told her about various constellations, and knew she wasn't bored. Life fascinated Meg; it was one of the many things about her that enchanted him.

Almost two hours later, while she was studying the moon again, he slipped his hands beneath the robe and caressed her bare skin.

"Daniel," she said, a hint of laughter in her voice, "that's not part of celestial observation."

"Maybe not in your opinion," he said, kissing the side of her neck. "But I know a heavenly body when I see it."

She laughed, and he swung her up into his arms and carried her inside.

THEY DIDN'T HEAD straight to the bedroom. He made them coffee, then put several brownies on a plate and carried it all into the front room. Late at night, the isolated ranch seemed like a safe ship floating on a dark sea. The dogs rested comfortably at their feet as they drank their coffee and talked. And Meg felt totally content. She didn't want to think too hard about tomorrow; she just wanted to feel and enjoy this moment, this night.

"It's a gorgeous plate," she said, admiring the rose-patterned china. "But it doesn't seem like you."

"It was my mother's," he admitted.

She waited for him to go on, comfortable in the silence. The plate didn't seem like Erna Willett's, either. If the woman had possessed an eye for beauty, she'd hidden it well while Meg had been around.

"When I tore down the old house," Daniel began slowly, "there were a lot of boxes and a few trunks in the attic. I put them all in storage, then transferred them back to this house when it was finished."

He was silent for a moment, but she didn't fill the quiet. She simply waited, knowing he was searching for the right words. He wanted to tell her, she sensed that much.

"All of it went into one corner of the garage. That door off the kitchen. During one winter, I brought it all in, a box at a time. One trunk, then the other. I searched through it all, disposed of what was junk, fixed what was worthwhile. Gave some away. Cleaned up a lot of it. Repair work, mostly." He took another sip of his coffee.

She did the same, then reached for a brownie. These had been baked by a woman named Ginnie, a newcomer to Blue Spruce who lived in town above the local card shop. Despite her aversion for all the women who baked for Daniel, Meg had to admit these brownies were outstanding. She took one bite, then another, caught up in Daniel's story.

"I found some photo albums. A few journals." He paused. "I didn't think it was wrong to read them, because she was gone. I thought about reading them and then destroying all of it—not the pictures but the journals."

She nodded her head. The first night they'd met, at Duffy's, she'd sensed Daniel had achieved a certain kind of peace concerning the woman Erna had been. He'd done this, and had let her go. The woman's memory no longer had the power to hurt him in any way.

"I saw another side of my mother. The mother I re-membered as a small child. She was happy here for a short time, Meg. But she was scared. She didn't like living on the ranch. It was a different time, and mighty isolated for a woman."

"I can sympathize with that," she said carefully. Daniel had never talked as much in one stretch. She intuitively sensed that he hadn't discussed this with anyone else. And he needed to get it out.

"She had troubles. It was hard for her to give birth to us. She wanted a daughter desperately, but all she got were boys."

"Oh, Daniel." Her heart ached for him, making a discovery like that. It couldn't have been easy.

"She had a stillborn baby. Between Joe and Brett."

She knew, a heartbeat before he said it.

"A little girl."

She closed her eyes.

"I think it ate away at her," Daniel said quietly. "She wrote in those pages that if only she'd lived in town, maybe the doctor could have helped her. But it was the middle of winter, the roads were snowed in. My father helped her, but the baby was born dead."

Meg chanced a look at him, saw the tightness in his face, the bleak expression in his eyes.

"I think that's when it started coming apart for her. The writing... It was different. Sometimes it didn't even make any sense. Some of it... I was going to ask you if you might...if you had the time—"

"I'll look at it, Daniel. I'll tell you what I think."

They sat in silence for a time, until he spoke.

"I knew, as a child, that she was confused. I just

didn't know why. I wondered why she didn't do the basic things that other mothers did for their families. But she couldn't."

"Your father loved her," Meg said, pushing the words past her throat. It hurt, constricted so tightly against the emotion she felt. She didn't want to cry. Not right now.

"He did. He never let her down—"

He stopped, and she knew the unspoken ending to that sentence. Knew what had happened in this household after Bob Willett's death, because Alec had told her some of it.

"She blamed him, didn't she?"

"She wasn't very strong," he answered. "Some people just aren't."

"She blamed you, too." Meg knew he had to let this out, had to talk about it with someone he trusted.

He nodded his head.

"Alec told me." She reached out, put her hand over his. "It was like after your father died, she didn't want any of you."

"I think," Daniel said slowly, "that if she'd thought she could have survived, she would've walked off this ranch and never looked back."

Silence. There was nothing she could say, because it was the truth.

She hesitated, then said it. "It might have been better for all of you if she had."

He sighed, then covered his eyes with his free hand, his head tipped back against the comfortable chair.

She didn't say anything, but kept her hand on his, knowing he was on shaky emotional ground and was certainly too proud a man to break down in front of her.

He regained control slowly, sat up, took another sip of coffee.

"I organized all her things that winter. Then, late the following summer, I asked Alec, Joe and Brett to come out. I told them to take whatever they wanted. Anything they wanted to remember her by."

She hesitated, then had to ask. "Did they take anything?"

"A few things. Joe, especially. He wanted them for his home. Something to pass on to his girls, to give them a sense of family. But I don't know if he's told his wife the entire truth."

"Did they want to look at her journals?"

"No."

She thought about this. The other three Willett boys had lit out of town, leaving their memories behind. *No, not quite like that*, she silently corrected herself. She knew, better than anyone, how memories clung to a person. You carried certain things that happened to you wherever you went, no matter what occurred later in life.

Unless you could let it go. And forgive.

"How do you feel about her now, Daniel?" She kept her voice low. Quiet. She'd sat back, broken their physical contact. He needed the distance right now.

"Something happened to me when I read those journals. I felt as if...I understood her a little better. My mother was a fear biter."

"A what?"

"When you find an animal that's been mistreated...damaged emotionally...sometimes they won't let you get close to them. Or just so close, but no closer. No real connection. And if they get cornered, or *feel* cornered, it doesn't matter if you've fed them and cared for them for years. They'll turn on you. Revert to biting out of fear. They can't be changed."

She glanced over at the dogs, curled up in front of the fireplace, fast asleep.

He seemed to read her thoughts.

"Molly had been loved somewhere along the line. Enough so she was able to come out of her fear and trust me."

She nodded her head, understanding.

"And I had my father. You have no idea how grateful I was to him. For him."

"I know," she whispered. "Me, too." She sat up, took another sip of the now warm coffee to clear the tightness in her throat. "You know, Daniel, I liked him the minute I saw him."

"He liked you, too."

"He did?" She'd known it all along, but loved hearing it from Daniel.

"He thought you were a real little firecracker. That was his nickname for you when you weren't around. Miss Firecracker."

She smiled.

"And she was always better when you were around," he said, referring to his mother.

"I thought she was lonely, but...I had no idea."

"I heard her talking with my father one night, telling him how lucky your mother was, to have you for a daughter."

That brought a flash of painful memories. Meg said nothing, not wanting the conversation to head in that direction.

"You helped my family a lot, Meg."

In answer, she set her coffee down, got up from her chair and bridged the short distance to him. She sat down in his lap, put her arms around him, and rested her head on his shoulder.

"I always wished I could move in and bake you cakes. Clean things up. Help you." She hesitated, then plunged ahead. "Daniel, I knew your mother was in trouble, but I always sensed that if she could have been different, she would have been. She wanted to be, but she was scared. She just didn't know how."

"I know."

His arms were so tight around her, she could scarcely breathe. What she had to say next was difficult for her to admit, but she wanted to get it out.

"My mother—she could do it all, she just didn't want to. She didn't want me around. I've thought a lot about it, and I'm sure I was a mistake. Or maybe a calculated risk she engineered to hold on to my dad."

"What happened to him, Meg?"

"He left when I was three. Didn't want to see either of us again, or so she told me. I was supposed to be a boy, anyway."

"She told you that?"

"Once when we were fighting. I wasn't an easy child to raise, Daniel."

"I'll bet she told you that, too."

"More than once." She settled more snugly against his chest, seeking comfort. "I wondered why she was the way she was for so many years. Your dad finally put that to rest."

"He loved people for who they really were. He recognized and accepted their shortcomings."

"He was terrific. I think I wrote my novel about him. About...all of you. You have no idea how you all affected me."

"Have you forgiven her, Meg?"

She knew who Daniel was referring to.

"I don't think... I haven't... No."

He gathered her closer, his chin resting on her head.

"I know I have to do it, sooner or later."

"Don't push yourself. You don't have a set of her journals, and something tells me you never will."

So like his daddy, she thought. Straight to the point, when truth was the kindest way to help a person heal.

"Maybe you could write a book about it," he said.

"I am." She wasn't even surprised that he'd guessed her intentions. She and Daniel had always had a connection, and she'd taken it for granted. Never again.

"Good."

They sat together, comfortably silent. Sensing the conversation had reached its natural end, Meg decided to change the subject. Lighten the mood.

"You never did take me skinny-dipping, Cowboy."

"The night is young."

"Daniel!"

"Tomorrow morning, I promise."

"Tomorrow afternoon?" She looked up at him from beneath her lashes. "I'm kind of tired."

He smiled down at her, then kissed the tip of her nose.

"Whatever you want."

HE LET HER SLEEP IN, then took her on a complete tour of the ranch. He showed her his three Arabians, and she found she loved his horses. Their fiery, spirited temperaments enchanted her, as did the equine intelligence she read in their liquid eyes.

The two black-and-white goats made her laugh with their antics, and he let her throw some feed for the chickens.

Then they set off on their adventure.

They reached the pond on Daniel's property a little after noon. The sun rode high in the sky, bright and hot as Meg slipped out of her jeans and House of Blues T-shirt and hung them on a nearby bush.

"At least Joe or Brett isn't here to steal our clothing."

"They told you about that?"

She wiggled her eyebrows at him. "You have no idea the family secrets I know."

Then she was racing toward the water, screaming, as he chased her. She ran in, and the cold shock of the pond even on this hot day made her yelp. He caught her around the waist and pulled her under.

They surfaced, sputtering, as she swiped her hair off her face.

"No fair!"

"All's fair," he said, then kissed her.

When they finally parted, she whispered, "I thought cold water was supposed to have a certain-effect—"

"Not with you around."

She laughed and splashed him. A water fight of monumental proportions ensued until he caught her and carried her up the bank toward the blanket he'd spread out earlier.

"YOU," HE SAID almost an hour later, "are a little pagan."

"You think so?" She stretched, relishing the feel of the sunlight and cool breeze on her damp, naked body. They lay close together on the cotton blanket, resting. He'd let her sleep late this morning, and shower alone, so she should have been expecting what had just happened.

"Let's see," she said. "In my bed, in the barn, in the shower and on the floor..." She slanted him what she knew was a mischievous look. "Where did 'by the pond' come in?"

"I'm great at improvising."

She laughed. "How about on the porch?"

"The day is young, Blue."

They laughed and talked. Shared the picnic lunch they'd both created in the kitchen. Hunter had ridden in the truck with them, and now begged for pieces of chicken from their sandwiches. Lying beneath the trees, they finished up their lunch with a few more of the brownies, along with the last of a thermos of lemonade.

Satiated, Meg turned to say something to Daniel and was startled by the intense expression in his dark gray eyes.

"Meg," he began.

She waited, holding her breath so tightly her chest hurt.

"Stay here—for the rest of the week."

She let it out. "Yes." She'd wanted to, but never would have considered it if he hadn't brought it up. She would stay with him for the rest of her life if he asked, but she wasn't sure he would. Something still seemed to hold Daniel back, and she felt she almost knew what it was.

"Yes," she said again, then went into his arms.

10

STAY HERE. WHAT DID Daniel's words really mean?

Meg thought of this as she carefully mixed chocolate-chip cookie dough Wednesday morning. Laura had come through for her as a true, nonjudgmental friend. Meg had phoned her earlier and told her she would be there this afternoon for lunch—right after Susie's appointment—and that she would be picking up all her stuff and staying with Daniel for the rest of the week.

"Are you ever going to let me in on what's going on?" Laura had asked.

"How can I, when I'm not sure?" Meg hurriedly had changed the subject. "What I need from you now is your grandmother's killer recipe for chocolate-chip cookies."

"They are the best," Laura had said immodestly.

Meg had figured she could make up the dough with what Daniel had in his cupboard, then pick up some cookie sheets and chocolate chips on the way out of town, after lunch. She was so busy mixing the basic dough she didn't hear Daniel come into the house until he spoke.

"BLUE? I THOUGHT YOU had a deadline for that book."
He came into the kitchen, opened the refrigerator and

took out a jug of apple juice. After pouring himself a glass, he leaned against the counter and surveyed the mess.

Meg looked...frazzled. She had a touch of flour on her nose, and she was beating whatever was in that bowl as if it were alive.

"Only in my head. I'm stuck in the middle, it's sagging badly, so I thought if I got away from work and did something totally unrelated to structuring the darn thing, something might gel."

He nodded. She might have been talking Swahili for all he understood. But if she was happy, that was all that mattered to him. After all, he'd gotten her to stay the week. Surely he could ask her to consider the rest of her life?

"Oh," she said as he started out the door. He stopped. "Daniel, I'm headed into town for lunch with Laura and Heather. And Susie, of course. I shouldn't be long."

"Do you need any help getting your things?"

"Nope. Though I was kind of getting fond of this particular outfit."

He laughed as she indicated the faded blue jeans and House of Blues T-shirt. She'd dutifully washed out her underwear every night, and he'd enjoyed seeing those delicate bits of nylon and lace hanging in his bathroom.

"I was, too." He thought for a moment. "I'm low on dog food. Could you pick up a forty-pound bag at the feed store? I'm sure Mike could load it into the car for you."

"No problem." She wrinkled her nose, furrowed her forehead as she stared at the bowl.

"What are you making?"

"Chocolate-chip cookies."

"My favorite," he said.

"I know."

He peeked in the bowl, hoping for a taste of the dough. "I don't see any chips."

"Oh, I'm picking them up on the way back. Along with some cookie sheets. Your kitchen is lacking in the cookie-baking department."

"I haven't done much baking lately."

"You haven't had to." She stuck out her tongue, and he laughed.

"SUSIE, YOUR HAIR LOOKS great," Meg said.

"Thank you," Laura answered. "I knew the job was dangerous when I took it."

Meg took another look at Susie, who sat across from her at the small table on Laura's porch. Laura had given Susie the complete treatment. Off had come three inches of frizzled, damaged ends. Her hair had been deep conditioned so it no longer resembled straw, and the brassy blond color had been toned down. Now Susie looked at least five years younger.

Laura had also shaped her eyebrows, sold her a few new items of makeup, and Minnie had done her nails.

"I feel like a brand-new girl," Susie said. She turned her attention to Meg. "So, what's the scoop on you and Daniel? Talk's spreading through town like a brush-fire."

"There's nothing— We haven't—"

"Save it, Meg," Heather said dryly. "Everyone saw

his pickup outside your motel room. The news hit Duffy's like a tornado by eleven that same night."

Meg leaned back in her chair, determined to bluff it out. "He saw me back to my room. I had a bad crick in my neck. He helped me find my heating pad, and stayed with me for a while."

Susie smiled, not unkindly. "That must have been quite a crick. Cindy Hellerman saw him leave the parking lot at around five in the morning. She was clearing off one of her tables in the coffee shop."

Unfortunately, Meg remembered, the coffee shop in The Aspen Motel was open twenty-four hours. And had large glass windows that faced the parking lot.

"Well," she said. She paused, then cleared her throat. "Okay, he did spend the night. But nothing happened." At least that much was the truth. Saturday night, nothing *had* happened between them. They'd gone straight to sleep like a comfortable, long-married couple. Now, Sunday morning...

"Really?" Susie seemed disappointed.

"You know," Heather said, "I believe her. Daniel's one of the last true gentlemen left in Blue Spruce."

"So I hear," Susie said, taking another long swig of her iced tea. "You had to import a guy all the way from Denver. How's that going?"

"Just fine. We're going away for a few days tomorrow."

"Lucky you!" Susie said. "Where?"

"Las Vegas. Some kind of computer convention or something. But I've never been, so I'm excited."

Meg watched Heather, admiring her friend. Heather was, hands down, the coolest and calmest of them all.

Hypersensitive, she hated conflict and would do anything to avoid it. Her goal in life seemed to be to make sure things went smoothly.

An impeccably tasteful dresser, with a management job at Blue Spruce's local bank, Heather had quite a nest egg of her own. She was the only person Meg knew who never ran out of money, and didn't have an inheritance or trust fund to back herself with.

Her life seemed cool, serene and unruffled, compared to the tumult simmering just beneath the surface of Meg's own emotional state.

"You girls," Susie said, playing with her new, shoulder-length hair. "You don't know how exciting it is for me to hear about your wild lives. A takeout pizza and a two-for-one movie coupon at Murphy's Drugstore and Video with Kevin once the kids are in bed is about as exciting as it gets at my house."

"That sounds wonderful," Laura said, a hint of wistfulness in her voice. "You have a great guy there, Susie."

"Well, I like him."

The lunch continued, with laughter and gossip. Then, by prearranged agreement, both Heather and Laura left the table at the far end of the porch. Meg finally found her time alone with Susie, and knew she had to tell her the truth.

"Susie, I need to tell you something really important."

Susie leaned forward. "If it's about Daniel, I promise I won't tell a soul. Sometimes it's just good to talk. You know, let it all out."

Strangely enough, Meg believed her. Susie had

never been the gossipy type. She just liked to live vicariously through her still-single girlfriends. This was not a woman who would ever betray a confidence.

"No, it's not about Daniel. It's about the award."

It took Susie a moment to switch gears, then she blossomed again. "Wasn't it just beautiful, that little woman with a pen? I looked at so many before I chose that one, but I just knew—"

"Susie, I can't accept it."

"What?"

Now Meg knew how the hunter who killed Bambi's mother would have felt if he'd possessed a conscience. Susie looked stricken, as if her entire world were caving in around her.

"Meg, you can't—"

"Susie," Meg said, taking the woman's hand, squeezing it reassuringly. "I'm trusting you with my life here, and I need you to listen to what I'm about to tell you. And if you ever tell anyone, I'll come back and find you."

Susie nodded her head, almost struck dumb.

Swiftly, as economically as possible, Meg told her the truth. About that long-ago vacation. The photos Laura had taken. The story that had spiraled out of control. Her nonexistent mansion. Her inability to sell novels two and three. And finally, the way she felt about her life right now.

"That's awful!" Susie said. "Those people in New York are fools!"

"Thanks. But can't you see how I'd feel like a total phony, taking that award home with me?"

Susie didn't answer right away, which surprised

Meg. She leaned back in her chair and stared out over the lake. Then she finally spoke.

"I don't think you're a phony," she said quietly.

"But Susie—"

"No, hear me out. And I hope I can find the right words to tell you what you mean to me. What you did. Nobody in Blue Spruce ever did what you did, Meg, and you have no idea what it meant to us. I really don't think you do."

Meg sat back in her chair.

"I graduated from high school and married Kevin." Susie pulled her chair a little closer to Meg's. "Did it mostly to get out of the house. Had two kids and I swore I'd never treat them like my dad treated me. I'm not saying that I regret any of my choices. I love Kevin, and I love my kids."

"I know," Meg said.

"But sometimes— I don't know, there's not a lot for a woman here. I do my work, and I never feel as if I'm caught up, and there's never enough money at the end of the month, and I never feel as if I spend enough time with the kids—" She paused, but Meg didn't say anything. Susie was clearly searching for words.

"It's like I knew I was giving up something the day I got married. But I wanted to. I didn't have that—that burning thing you had inside you, Meg. But I wanted you to do something like what you did. For all of us." Susie swung her gaze away from the lake and pinned Meg with it. "Am I making any sense at all?"

"You sure are."

"What a woman does... It's like it isn't noticed. Or it isn't understood, or something. But when I read your book, and I got inside all those people and I lived with them for a while..." Susie hesitated. "Damn, I wish I had your way with words."

Meg felt as if she knew what her friend was about to say, but she didn't want to take the words from her.

"It was like I *knew* them. I *knew* what Matthew went through, giving up so much. He did it because he wanted to, and in the end he won. And I was inside his head, so in the end, I won, too. You know?"

Meg nodded.

"So don't you *dare* sit here and tell me you're a failure! If all you ever did in your life was write that one book, it would be enough for me. And if you don't take that award back with you, I'm gonna hit you over the head with it."

"That won't be necessary," Laura said. She and Heather had come up behind Meg without her noticing. "I think she'll take it home."

"She will if she knows what's good for her," Heather added.

"How did I get so lucky," Meg said, looking at the women surrounding her, "to have friends like you?"

SHE WENT TO THE LOCAL market and found the chocolate chips and cookie sheets. She also bought a hot-air popper and some gourmet popcorn. Then, using Daniel's card, she stopped at the video store and rented a movie. An evening at home, snuggled up in bed and watching a romantic comedy didn't sound half bad. If they started early enough, Daniel would be able to see the whole thing.

Then she went to Mike's Feed Store and all hell broke loose.

Mike had just rung up the forty-pound bag of dog food and she'd whipped out her credit card when she heard a voice behind her say, "I just hope she doesn't fool around with that young man and break his heart. Bob Willett was a fine man, and his son should know better."

Meg remained perfectly still for a second, then handed Mike her card with a shaky hand. Her first decision was to simply ride it out, to pretend she hadn't heard. She was accustomed to that sort of hostility, but at least in Los Angeles it was veiled. Blue Spruce didn't seem to have that sort of sophistication.

"Martha, settle down," said a weary male voice.

Jake Bodine. Meg recognized that voice. A genuinely nice man, married to a nasty old harpy. Paula, with another twenty years of bitterness piled on.

"Well, it's true. Ask anyone around town. She comes back like the Queen of Sheba, takes up with one of the best men around, then just you wait! She'll leave, and break his heart all over again. Just like she did before."

"Martha, please—"

Meg took her card back from Mike, quietly asked him to carry the dog food to her car, then started outside.

"Just like her mother. I tell you, the nut doesn't fall far from the tree."

Tears blurred her vision. It did no good to tell herself that Martha Bodine was an unhappy woman who took her nastiness out on whoever was in her way. She'd just been ahead of her in line at the feed store, and the woman liked to hear herself talk.

"Don't pay her no mind, Meg," Mike said as he swung the dog food into the back seat of the rental sedan. Meg would have used the trunk, but it was full of all her stuff, her clothes and her laptop. "She's always given everyone hell. Most of all, poor Jake."

"Thanks, Mike." She got in the car, started it up, then turned out onto the highway toward Daniel's ranch, wiping at the tears on her face.

BETTY BICKHAM HAD finally had enough.

"Martha Bodine," she said, her voice loud and clear, carrying through Mike's Feed Store, "you're a sorry old fool!"

"What!" the woman said, turning on her.

"Why, anyone with eyes in their head knows those two have been in love with each other since high school. So why in the name of blazes did you have to say what you just said?"

"She's not good enough for him—"

"She's perfect for Daniel. Absolutely perfect. And you should have your mouth washed out with lye soap for the way you talked to her just now."

"Her mother—"

"Her mother had nothing to do with this. I don't care what sort of problem you had with Antonia Prescott, but don't you ever let me catch you taking out your holier-than-thou judgments on Meg again."

"Jake!" Martha screeched. "Are you going to let her talk to me that way?"

Jake smiled, then shrugged his shoulders. "It's the

truth. The girl's got nothing to do with the mother. She's not like her."

Martha stormed out of the store as Jake quietly paid for his purchases and headed out to their pickup.

In the meantime, Betty headed for the pay phone at the back of the store. Sometimes, she thought as she dialed Daniel's number, romance needed more than a vase of flowers. Sometimes, it just needed a helping hand.

MEG CAME INTO THE ranch house quietly and dumped her two grocery bags on the kitchen counter. Daniel had risen from his chair by the fireplace and headed toward the kitchen when he'd heard the crunch of her tires on the gravel drive.

"Good lunch?" he asked.

"Very nice."

He could sense the fine tension in her. He'd been feeding the dogs when Betty had called and filled him in on the scene at the feed store. Although everyone in town recognized Martha Bodine for the mean-spirited woman she was, he still knew how Meg must have taken it.

"Anything wrong?"

She turned a stiffly smiling face toward him. "No. You?"

He stepped back a little. Gave her some space. "Nope. Nice popcorn popper," he commented as she unloaded the first bag.

"I thought we could watch a movie tonight. I rented one, do you mind?"

"No, that'd be fine." He felt as if he were navigating

a minefield. "I took some soup out of the freezer this morning for supper. Is that all right with you, or would you like something different? We could defrost some steaks."

"Soup's fine."

But she wasn't, and he watched her, his heart heavy, as she left the kitchen and walked out onto the porch.

YOU WILL NEVER FIT IN here. People will never forget.

She'd been on such a high after her lunch with Susie that the incident at the feed store had come at her like a punch to her stomach. Painful. Humiliating.

She wasn't sure she could put Daniel through it.

Was that how the town saw the two of them? Bob Willett's son was practically Blue Spruce royalty, while she was just an upstart who'd had the misfortune to have Antonia Prescott, super snob, for a mother.

Meg walked over to the porch railing and stared out toward the mountains. Dusk was fast approaching, and she watched the play of light over the stark rock formations. The peaceful view did little to soothe her feelings. And she thought, not for the first time since she'd been back, about how ironic her situation was. And how the townspeople would be astonished if they knew how little a relationship she had with her mother.

She'd flown to New York shortly after her first novel had been released, to talk with her editor and solidify her fledgling career. And at the same time, as she hadn't heard from her mother, she thought she would try to see her. Antonia had never been one to encourage visits, so Meg had decided, in a rebellious mood, to just drop in on her. Not terribly polite, she knew, but looking back, she realized she hadn't wanted to give her mother a chance to put her off with another excuse.

Her mother's address took Meg to the Upper East Side, and after the doorman had a brief conversation with Antonia, Meg found herself in an opulent elevator, on her way up to the twenty-seventh floor.

Standing in the doorway of the lavish apartment, Antonia didn't look pleased. She did look good. Stylishly dressed, with perfect makeup and stunning jewelry, she studied her daughter for a long, uncomfortable moment before letting her inside.

Meg gripped the railing of Daniel's porch. Remembering. Feeling emotion wash over her.

Their conversation had been brief and uncomfortable. In retrospect, Meg couldn't remember any of it. Her mother hadn't offered her anything to drink, hadn't made any move toward making her feel comfortable or like she wanted her to stay.

Meg had deliberately walked past the elegant foyer and into the large living room, with its exquisite antiques and spectacular view of Central Park. She hadn't really seen any of it; she just didn't want her mother to send her away. For some reason, this time she wanted to get to the bottom of things.

And then she'd seen the pictures.

Martin, Antonia's husband, was a stunningly handsome man, with thick, silvery hair and piercing blue eyes. Groupings of photos, in their expensive silver frames, graced shelves, small tables and the mantel of the large fireplace. Meg searched for one of herself— from any time in her life—and found none.

And then she knew.

Slowly, not wanting to accept what was literally staring her in the face, she turned toward her mother.

"You haven't— He doesn't know about me." She phrased it as a statement, not a question.

Antonia remained perfectly calm, not a hair out of place. "No. He doesn't."

And Meg realized that her mother had probably tossed her novel as soon as she'd opened the package. That Antonia would never do anything to jeopardize her meal ticket. Ever. It didn't matter what Martin's opinions on the subject might have been, the woman had abdicated her role of mother when she'd swiftly packed her suitcases and left Blue Spruce.

Meg could never quite remember what she'd said after that, or how she'd left the apartment. She'd simply stumbled into the elevator, stood with her nails digging into her palms as she'd watched the blurred numbers descend. Then had gone out into the lobby, ignoring the doorman's cheerful greeting, and out the front door into the frigid, February afternoon.

What she did remember, oddly enough, was the cab she'd hailed not less than half a block from Antonia's apartment. In New York, that was nothing less than miraculous.

"Where to?" he'd said.

"Just drive. Please." *Away from here...*

He'd gone a few miles before she spotted a coffee shop.

"Over there."

She'd handed him a few crumpled bills, stepped out of the cab onto the slushy curb, then into the steamy warmth of the shop. The hostess, an older woman, had taken one look at her face and directed her toward a back booth.

"Tea," Meg had said quietly, her voice breaking. She'd cleared her throat, willed herself to be strong. "I'll start with tea."

The coffee shop hadn't been crowded, and she'd been thankful. She'd sat in that cracked vinyl booth, stirring lots of sugar and lemon into her tea, staring out at the street where it had started to sleet.

And she'd known she would never contact her mother again.

HIS HEART ACHED FOR HER as he watched her standing out on the porch, probably not even seeing his Arabians in the corrals. The sun was just starting to go down, and ordinarily he would have walked out onto the porch to share the sunset with her. But he sensed she needed some time alone, and gave it to her.

Later they ate their soup. Popped popcorn and watched the movie. He held her in his arms the entire time, but it was as if she wasn't there. Her sparkle had gone.

Much later, as he watched her sleep, a sad, regretful thought entered his mind.

She may never fit in here. Some people choose not to forget.

He hadn't thought she would want to make love. She'd been too upset for him to even suggest it. After the video, she'd made a production of how terribly tired she was.

He knew her so well. If they'd started to make love, if he'd opened her up emotionally, she would have cried and told him about the entire incident. She obviously wanted to keep it to herself for a little longer.

As he'd worked in the barn this afternoon, he'd planned out how he was going to ask her to stay forever. Marriage, children, the whole works. He'd actually decided this morning, when he'd seen that smudge of flour on her nose.

Now, as he lay in the dark bedroom, his arms around her, Daniel realized that Betty's phone call had finally given him a clear picture of just exactly how much he was asking her to sacrifice.

THE FOLLOWING MORNING, a ringing phone brought Meg out of a deep, life-evading sleep.

"Are you sitting down?" Laura asked.

"I'm *lying* down," Meg said, trying to orient herself. If she'd had her way, she would have spent today beneath the covers. Mornings weren't her best time of day, anyway.

"Well, get ready for a stunner! Heather eloped, and her mom's going ballistic!"

"Heather? Eloped?" She thought quickly. "Las Vegas? Donald?"

"You got it. Boy, was she the cool one at lunch!"

Meg smiled, sat up in bed and ruffled her hair to clear her head. "Good for her! She's got more guts than I have."

"Same here."

LATER THAT SAME afternoon, the ink cartridge in her rented printer ran out.

"I won't be gone long," she told Daniel. "I'm just going to run into town and get another one at the stationer's. Do you want me to pick up anything?"

"No. Can't think of a thing."

She was avoiding him and she could tell he knew it. Well, she would force herself to talk to him when she came back home. Something had to be decided. And soon.

MINNIE WAS AT THE stationer's, halfheartedly sorting through several birthday cards.

"Minnie!" Meg said, genuinely glad to see her. "How are you? I love your nails!" Today's shade was a glowing orange-red.

"Cheyenne Pepper. You should come in for a manicure, Meg. I can always fit you in." Minnie hesitated. "Would you help me pick out a birthday card for my mother-in-law? You have such exquisite taste. That mansion—"

Now or never, Prescott.

"I don't have a mansion, Minnie. I never did."

"Huh?" Now the young woman seemed confused. "But I saw the pictures—"

"The Beverly Hills Hotel. Sunset Boulevard. Beautiful place, but much too expensive for me." At that moment, Meg knew she'd already decided she couldn't stay in Blue Spruce. It would be like asking her to walk a tightrope she couldn't possibly stay on.

She would never come back again. Couldn't bear to. So she might as well blow the whole facade of being filthy rich sky-high. Once and for all.

"But Meg—"

"It's a hotel, Minnie. Lots of people live there, but I have a one-bedroom apartment in West Hollywood."

"But you wrote a book—"

"Yep. Got a lousy advance and couldn't give away novels two and three."

"But Meg—"

And then she saw it. Laura and Heather had been right. People didn't want to give up their dreams—their illusions—about how they thought the world operated. Minnie *wanted* her to live in a gracious mansion in Beverly Hills, and that was all there was to it.

"No mansion, Minnie. There never was, and never will be—"

"Well, look who's here. Little Miss Filthy Rich herself."

Meg glanced up and froze.

Paula.

IT WAS WAY PAST TIME to get out of Dodge.

Not relishing the thought of being pounded into the rust-colored carpet inside Greene's Stationery Store, Meg lit out the front door like an escaped con with bloodhounds on her heels. She ran down Main Street, Paula hot on her trail.

"You're not so brave now, without Daniel!" the woman yelled. And Meg had to marvel. Paula smoked at least a pack and a half per day. She certainly didn't do aerobics or weights. She probably didn't even take vitamins. And yet the woman could still run flat out and scream at her at the same time. While she, Miss Sit-on-Her-Butt-at-Her-Desk-All-Day, was already decidedly winded and would soon have a nasty stitch in her side.

She'd almost resigned herself to her fate when a familiar voice called out.

"Meg! Over here!"

Bruno, on his Harley, sat at the intersection of the two main streets in town. She blinked as sweat ran into her eyes, making them sting and causing Bruno to blur into a shimmering mirage.

"Bruno!" she wheezed, and with one last superhuman effort, Meg managed to dart out into the street, throw herself on the back of his motorcycle, and hang on for dear life as the light changed to green and he gunned the powerful motor.

CONFESSION WAS GOOD for the soul, but never in a million years would Meg have thought she would be sitting at Duffy's Tavern in the middle of a weekday, crying into her beer and confessing all to Bruno Delgado.

The amazing thing was, he proved to be an astounding listener—and totally nonjudgmental, but considering Bruno's wild past, he couldn't really afford to be. He never had been, anyway.

"Let me get this straight. You're crazy in love with the guy, he's told you he loves you, he's asked you to stay, you want to stay, but you're worried about wrecking his life because of what a couple of old farts in town think?"

Only Bruno could have summed things up so perfectly.

"Bruno, I'm a lot of trouble—"

"In a cute little package, if I do say so myself."

She had to laugh. A beer had helped loosen her up and had eased the tension considerably.

"Hey, Bruno knows best! Ba-da-bing, ba-da-bang, ba-da-*boom!* You'll make Daniel Willett one happy man, Meg. 'Cause he's been in love with you since high school."

That caught her attention. She stared at him so hard, she thought her bloodshot eyes might pop right out of her head.

Bruno stared right back, then swallowed. "You didn't *know?*" He scratched his head, suddenly uneasy. "Uh, did I just say something I shouldn't have?"

"Bruno, are you sure?"

"Sure? Everyone in town saw it. The only reason he didn't ask you to marry him—well, I mean, the way I figure it—was that he didn't want to tie you down. Hold you back. From being a big success, you know. Hey, about that mansion—"

Now was not the time to disillusion him.

"Bruno," she said, grabbing a fistful of his Harley-Davidson T-shirt. He had to have a closet of them at home, much the same way a banker had a wardrobe filled with conservative suits. "Bruno, backtrack to that little bit about how he's loved me—"

"Since high school."

"Yeah. That part. That was *lust*. He explained it all to me—"

"No. It might have started with lust, but with a guy like Daniel, it turned into love within about, oh, I'd say maybe an hour. Or two."

"Oh, my God." She took another swig of her beer and considered ordering a shot of tequila.

"Why do you think he was sitting on this barstool last Friday? To see how our class fared over the years? I think *not!*" Bruno slammed his beer bottle on the counter for emphasis.

"You tell 'em," a man farther down the counter mumbled, his head resting on his crossed arms.

Bruno's words had changed the picture, and for some reason Meg could see it all clearly now.

"Bruno, what would you do?"

"If I were you? Stay with the guy, get married, have a couple of bambinos, and write another one of those novels. Maybe a little something about girls in prison—you know what I mean? Now, about that mansion—"

"Bruno, wait right here." She grabbed her purse and headed toward the pay phone back in the corner by the rest rooms. There was one other person who would know. Who would have to have known, all those years ago.

Alec.

Now, if she could just remember where he lived...

One of her many gifts as a writer was an almost-photographic memory of events, both factual and emotional. She closed her eyes, picturing Duffy's as it had looked almost a week ago, crowded with people, purple and white balloons festooning the large room, glitter on the counters, laughter and talking and—

"What about Alec?"

"He's engaged to a girl from Atlanta. They live in Flagstaff."

Bingo.

She picked up the receiver.

IT DIDN'T TAKE HER LONG to track him down, and when she finally called, Alec was delighted to hear from her. Meg didn't indulge in small talk, but got straight to the point.

And Alec, like both his father and Daniel, told her the truth.

"Meg, he let us all fly free."

She was crying now, the tears running down her cheeks as she leaned against the wall and listened. Two different men had come up to use the phone, taken one look at her, and left.

"I was out there, late one summer. Saw what he did to the old house, and the new one he'd built. We were out by the corral, watching his first Arabian run. He compared you to that horse, Meg. Wild. Spirited and free, never to be broken. He didn't want a rancher's life for you."

She hadn't known, hadn't guessed. Would never have left him if she had. But he'd been so quiet, so private about his feelings.

"He thought being a rancher's wife would have broken you. Destroyed your dreams." Alec's voice thickened with emotion, and she heard him clear his throat. "And he didn't want you to have to deal with our mother. That wouldn't have been pleasant."

"Did he tell you about her journals, Alec?"

"Yeah."

"You should read them. Because—" She was crying so hard she could barely speak. "Because you're lucky to have them."

"Yeah. I know." He sighed. "Daniel was the one who had all the guts. Except when it came to you."

"Why? I would have stayed with him—"

"He knew that, Meg. *I* knew it. Absolutely, from the bottom of my soul. He knew you would have stayed, so he gave you no reason to."

"Oh, Alec—"

"You go get him, Miss Firecracker." She heard deep affection in his voice. "Don't let him talk you out of it. My brother's been lonely, all those winters on that ranch. He needs someone like you, *exactly* like you, to warm him up."

She laughed through her tears. "Thanks."

"Hey, I love you both. And though we would've killed each other if we'd tried for anything permanent, I can't think of anyone else I'd rather have as a sister-in-law."

"Thanks."

"Go get him, Meg." She could feel his hesitation over the long-distance line. "He needs you."

"I know. I need him."

"Tell him. Daniel needs to be needed."

"Okay."

"Tell him I'll whip his butt if he doesn't make an honest woman of you."

She said her goodbyes, walked back to Bruno's table, and eyed the shots of tequila he'd ordered for both of them.

"Just one," he said. "On me. For courage."

She knocked it back, then walked to the front door, out of the dimly lit tavern and into the late-afternoon sunshine.

11

DANIEL FINALLY HAD to shut Molly and Digger in the garage, after they'd both disgraced themselves by destroying part of the garden in their attempt to capture a rabbit. Now, at dusk, he was out in the barn. The Arabians were fed, the chickens and goats taken care of.

He'd also brought some food to the tiny, black feral cat who'd taken up residence high in the hay bales. He only hoped this particular feline wouldn't turn out to be a female and get pregnant before he could catch her and have her fixed.

Knowing Meg wasn't back inside the house, and knowing how lonely it felt without her presence, he sat down on a hay bale and ruffled Hunter's floppy, black-and-tan ears. She looked up at him and whined.

"You've had your supper, so I know you can't be hungry."

She whined again, then settled her chin on his jeans-clad leg. He marveled at her perception. She knew something was wrong, could sense it in him. Knew he'd struggled with a decision all late afternoon and into the evening, and had just about come to terms with it.

He'd decided to let Meg go.

"It's the way it has to be," he said, stroking the dog's soft head. "I want the best for her."

Hunter licked his hand.

"I sure wouldn't have chosen for it to turn out this way, but I can't bear to think of her hurting. Martha Bodine hurt her badly, and she'll hurt her again."

Hunter whined, then raised her head and glanced toward the barn door.

Daniel turned and saw her. Meg. Dressed in the same jeans and purple sweater she'd worn to go into town. But she looked a little worse for wear. Her hair stood up in spiky little clumps, her eyes were unnaturally bright and slightly bloodshot, her mascara smeared. She looked worn-out but there was a gleam in her eye he couldn't quite identify.

"Martha Bodine can stuff it," she said quite clearly.

He stood and started toward her. Then stopped, almost five feet away from her. She had been crying, he could see that now. She looked tired, as if she'd been walking a great many miles. Searching.

"Daniel," she said softly. "You have to ask me. A woman has to know."

His throat closed.

"I talked to Alec. He told me...he told me what you did. How you wanted me to...go." Now she looked him directly in the eye, and he could see fresh tears starting to spill down her cheeks. "I never would have left you, Cowboy."

He nodded his head. Still couldn't speak. He felt raw and naked. Ashamed. Of wanting her so much, of needing her in his life so badly. Of wanting to simply pick her up in his arms, carry her into his house and never let her go.

His house. He'd tried to create a home, but now he knew it would never be a home without Meg.

He watched her struggle to contain her emotions. The way those slender hands shook. The way her throat worked.

"I didn't know," she whispered. "Bruno told me...how you really felt about me. I knew you wanted to sleep with me, because I felt the same way about you. But I didn't know—"

"It wouldn't have worked," he said quietly. "You might have tried to stay, but I never would have blamed you if you'd left."

"Maybe. Maybe not. I was pretty immature back then. I really didn't know what was important." She raked an unsteady hand through her hair, causing the clumps to shift. And he remembered the first night of the reunion, how she'd sweated when she was nervous. She was nervous now.

So was he.

"You know about the feed store."

He saw no reason to lie. "Yes."

She hesitated, and he watched her struggle with that, all the time wishing he had the words, the ability to express all he was feeling. It would make things so much easier between them.

"I know I'm a little strange—"

"No." His voice broke on the word. He moved a little closer to her. "No."

Suddenly she seemed spent. "Daniel, I don't give a damn what they think, so long as you're not ashamed—"

"Never. Never, Blue. I was always proud of you."

She nodded her head. "Okay." She cleared her throat, stuck her hands in her jeans pockets, then took one back out and chewed nervously on a fingernail.

He wanted to ask her to stay like he'd wanted nothing else in his life.

"I don't think I can walk away again," she whispered.

He stared at her, willing his voice to work, trying to force the words past the tight lump in his throat.

Then she took those words, literally, right out of his mouth.

"*I'm lonely*, Daniel. Everyone thinks I'm having such a great time out there in Los Angeles, when the truth is there are days I'm so lonely I'm sick with it. And I try to go out and connect with a man, but I can't. Because the only man I want to be with is you, and you won't let me stay."

He put his hand over his eyes, hating the way they stung. He couldn't break down in front of her, but he had to look at her. Slowly, with great effort, he lowered his hand. No barriers between them. Not now.

"Daniel," she whispered. She reached across the few feet separating them. Almost touched him. Then lowered her hand, stared at her feet. The top of her head, those little spikes of blond hair, looked so terribly vulnerable.

Her voice was barely audible. "Daniel, you have to ask me, or I'll never be sure."

He knew what she meant.

Silence.

A part of him knew what he had to do.

Another part cried out inside him. Silently screamed, anguished.

She stood very still for almost a minute, then turned and began to walk out of the barn.

"Meg!" His voice didn't sound like his own. It seemed rusty, as if from lack of use.

Hunter whined.

She stopped, her back toward him.

"Meg, I— Please—"

He saw the absolute rigidity of her spine, and knew she would force herself out that barn door, off his property and out of his life forever if she thought that was what he truly wanted.

"Don't go."

She bowed her head, and he saw that delicate nape, the soft, warm skin he so loved to kiss in the morning.

"Meg," he said, reaching her side. He slid his arms around her. He couldn't see her face; she was turned away from him, her shoulders shaking.

Crying.

Then she turned in his arms, light as air, and pounded on his chest with her fists.

"*Say* it. I need to hear it."

He gripped her shoulders, pressed her against his chest, held her so tightly he thought he might be hurting her.

"Stay with me," he whispered, tears filling his eyes.

Her arms came up around his neck. He buried his face in her hair.

"Marry me," he whispered, as the tears finally fell.

She nodded her head. "Okay. Okay."

And finally, from that deepest, most hidden and

tender place in his heart came the words. "Don't leave me, Meg."

"Never," she said.

MUCH LATER THAT NIGHT, she climbed out of bed and went to his bookshelf by the stone fireplace. Finding her novel, she swiftly made her way back to the warmth of the bed, where she reached for the pen on the bedside table and turned the lamp to its lowest setting.

She opened the novel to its title page, and set pen to paper, knowing now what she wanted to write.

"To Daniel. I have loved you all my life. I'm so thankful we found each other again."

Then she set the pen down, closed the book and placed it gently on the bedside table. She slid back into bed, into Daniel's arms, now knowing that this was where she would be waking up every morning for the rest of her life.

When she reached to turn off the lamp, she noticed his eyes were slightly open.

"Did I wake you?"

He shook his head. "Hand me that book."

He read the dedication, and the emotion that filled his face almost made her start to cry. Then he turned off the light and she settled into his arms, next to his heart.

"I want you to know," he said, his breath warm against her ear, "that I've been a frugal man. I can afford a housekeeper for you."

"Daniel—"

"Don't argue with me, Blue." He took one of her

hands in his, linked their fingers. "I want these hands typing. Writing. Spinning those stories."

"Changing diapers."

He stilled, and she wondered if she'd simply stunned him. Then he turned the light back on and the expression in those gray eyes left her in no doubt that he wanted to take the entire journey with her.

"Maybe one of each," she said, kissing his neck and giving him a mischievous look. "A boy and a girl. Twins run on my mother's side of the family. Did you know that?"

Daniel simply threw back his head and laughed.

_____Epilogue_____

A mere three years later...

"OKAY EVERYBODY!" Meg called from the kitchen.

The Willett family was spread out all over the ranch house this late-June afternoon, the first time all four brothers had been together in quite some time. But it wasn't every day that Daniel Willett's one-year-old daughter, Emily, had a birthday.

Meg carefully carried the white sheet cake—adorned with light pink frosting, colorful sprinkles, animal crackers marching along the sides and a large pink-and-white candle on top—out to the porch where everyone was relaxing. She couldn't stop the smile that started deep inside her heart as she saw Daniel with Emily in his muscular arms. She looked absolutely adorable in the lacy white dress Laura had made for her.

Meg had felt a moment of panic in the hospital one year ago, when the doctor had told her and Daniel they had a little girl. What if Daniel secretly wanted a son? She'd looked up at him through tear-glazed eyes, so tired, so proud, so filled with joy.

He must have sensed her slight apprehension, because he leaned down, kissed her tenderly and whispered, "There are too many boys in the Willett family as it is. She's beautiful, Blue."

And Emily was. She loved her daddy, always had a smile and an infectious giggle for him. And Meg knew, with the deepest, most instinctual part of her heart, that something had been healed inside Daniel the day his daughter had been born. She knew, because that same emptiness had been filled within herself. They had truly become a family—the family both of them had searched for for years.

Everyone gathered around two picnic tables Daniel had pushed together for the occasion. Brett, still single and wickedly handsome. Joe, his wife, Robyn, and their two little girls. Alec and his wife, Michelle, who had once been the fiancée from Flagstaff. She was five months pregnant with their first child.

The dogs—Hunter, Digger and Molly—lazed underfoot, along with a mixed-breed puppy Daniel had found by a Dumpster in town. Sunny had become one of the family in no time. And Sluggo, Meg's elderly pug, had found his patch of warm sun on the far side of the porch, where he snored contentedly.

Meg had invited friends as well as family. Heather and Donald, Susie and Kevin. And Laura, still single but dating a really nice man named Scott. Their neighbor, Betty Sue from down the road, with her husband and children. Daniel had invited Betty Bickham and her husband Hal, and she'd brought enough flowers from her shop in town to fill several vases. Even Bruno Delgado, in his usual jeans and T-shirt with skull and crossbones, was present.

With the video camera in Brett's capable hands,

everyone sang the birthday song as Emily looked on, her attention captivated by the bright candle on her cake.

"You'll have to make a wish for her," Meg said to Daniel as he handed her their daughter.

He considered this, then blew out the single candle.

That evening, after their guests had left or were asleep for the night, and Emily was snug in her nursery with Hunter stationed protectively at the door, Meg sat out on the porch with Sluggo at her feet and her two cats curled up together on a nearby chair as she studied the stars.

She loved her home at this time of night: the familiar night rhythms of owls and mice, raccoons and possums. The wind whispering through the trees, the scents and sounds of evening. She didn't even have to look around to sense that Daniel was there, with Sunny tagging adoringly at his heels. Her husband sat down beside her on the porch swing and took her into his arms.

"One year old," he said.

"I know, I can't believe it's going this fast." She snuggled against him, totally content. "What did you wish for her, Daniel?"

"Happiness and love, all of her life."

"That's nice," she said.

"What would you have wished for her?"

"That we could always be as happy as we are right now."

He pulled her closer, rested his chin on top of her head. "Are you happy, Blue?"

She knew Daniel still sometimes worried that she

missed her fast-paced, former life. The classes and art galleries, the bookstores and coffeehouses. They went into Denver every few months, and she stocked up on reading material, gourmet coffee—and toys for Emily.

Meg had persevered with her writing. Her second novel, the one she'd started at The Aspen Motel, had sold four months ago and would be coming out next spring. A rebirth of sorts, she'd felt, on so many different levels.

But nothing on earth—not even her writing—compared to the love of this good man and the chance for them to raise their children in the shadow of the Rockies, beneath endless, starry skies. On their land. To create a home and make those loving connections that would heal and sustain them in the years ahead.

She'd told him this before, but knew that sometimes he had to hear it again. Because they'd both lost so much, and had come so close to losing each other.

Are you happy, Blue?

"Yes, Daniel," she said. "I am."

COMING NEXT MONTH

#758 BEAUTY & THE BEASTS • Janice Kay Johnson
Veterinarian Dr. Eric Bergstrom is interested in a new
woman. A *beautiful* woman. He's volunteered his services at
the local cat shelter she's involved with. He's even adopted
one of the shelter's cats. But he still can't manage to get
Madeline to go out with him. That's bad enough. Then Eric's
twelve-year-old son comes to town, making it clear that he
resents "having" to spend the summer with his father. Well,
at least Eric's new cat loves him....

#759 IN THE ARMS OF THE LAW • Anne Marie Duquette
Home on the Ranch
Morgan Bodine is part-owner of the Silver Dollar Ranch;
he's also the acting sheriff in Tombstone, Arizona.
Jasentha Cliffwalker is a biologist studying bats on Bodine
property. Morgan and Jaz loved each other years ago, but it
was a love they weren't ready for. *Are they ready now?*
They'll find out when a stranger comes to Tombstone,
threatening everything they value most.... By the author of
She Caught the Sheriff.

#760 JUST ONE NIGHT • Kathryn Shay
9 Months Later
Annie and Zach Sloan had married for all the right reasons.
They'd fallen in love and neither could imagine life without
the other. But those reasons hadn't been enough to keep
them together. Then—six years after the divorce—a night
that began in fear ended in passion. And now there's a
new reason for Zach and Annie to marry. *They're about to
become parents.*

#761 THIS CHILD IS MINE • Janice Kaiser
Carolina Prescott is pregnant. Webb Harper is the father.
After his wife died, he forgot all about the donation he'd left
at a fertility clinic. Due to a mix-up, Lina is given the wrong
fertilized egg—but that doesn't make her less of a mother!
Both Lina and Webb have strong feelings about the baby
she's carrying and the ensuing lawsuit. Can their growing
feelings for each other overcome the trauma of the battle
for custody?

Take 4 bestselling love stories FREE

Plus get a FREE surprise gift!

FORTUNE COOKIE

Breathtaking romance is predicted in your future with Harlequin's newest collection: Fortune Cookie.

Three of your favorite Harlequin authors, Janice Kaiser, Margaret St. George and M.J. Rodgers will regale you with the romantic adventures of three heroines who are promised fame, fortune, danger and intrigue when they crack open their fortune cookies on a fateful night at a Chinese restaurant.

Join in the adventure with your own personalized fortune, inserted in every book!

Don't miss this exciting new collection!

Available in September wherever Harlequin books are sold.

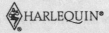

HARLEQUIN®

HARLEQUIN WOMEN KNOW ROMANCE WHEN THEY SEE IT.

And they'll see it on **ROMANCE CLASSICS**, the new 24-hour TV channel devoted to romantic movies and original programs like the special **Romantically Speaking—Harlequin™ Goes Prime Time.**

Romantically Speaking—Harlequin™ Goes Prime Time introduces you to many of your favorite romance authors in a program developed exclusively for Harlequin® readers.

Watch for **Romantically Speaking—Harlequin™ Goes Prime Time** beginning in the summer of 1997.

If you're not receiving ROMANCE CLASSICS, call your local cable operator or satellite provider and ask for it today!

ROMANCE CLASSICS

Escape to the network of your dreams.

See Ingrid Bergman and Gregory Peck in *Spellbound* on Romance Classics.

HARLEQUIN®
Temptation.

FOUR BRIDES:
Page, Blair, Keely & Emilie

TWO WORDS:
"We Don't!"

BRIDES ON THE RUN

A spirited Temptation heroine who's ready to say
"I do!" but ends up saying "I don't!"

Watch for the concluding book:

#653 THE BRIDE RODE WEST
by Kristine Rolofson, October 1997

NEW ORLEANS KNIGHTS

JoAnn Ross

**Three Brothers,
Three Heroes,
Three unforgettable Temptation novels
that will make you stay up past your bedtime...
then dream all through the night....**

Don't miss the last book in this amazing series.

MICHAEL: THE DEFENDER #654

Available in October 1997
wherever Harlequin books are sold.

HARLEQUIN®

Temptation

Look us up on-line at: http://www.romance.net

NOK

 **Free Gift Offer**

With a Free Gift proof-of-purchase
from any Harlequin® book, you can receive
a beautiful cubic zirconia pendant.

This stunning marquise-shaped stone is a genuine cubic
zirconia—accented by an 18" gold tone necklace.
(Approximate retail value $19.95)

Send for yours today...
compliments of ✦ HARLEQUIN®

To receive your free gift, a cubic zirconia pendant, send us one original proof-of-purchase, photocopies not accepted, from the back of any Harlequin Romance®, Harlequin Presents®, Harlequin Temptation®, Harlequin Superromance®, Harlequin Intrigue®, Harlequin American Romance®, or Harlequin Historicals® title available at your favorite retail outlet, together with the Free Gift Certificate, plus a check or money order for $1.65 U.S./$2.15 CAN. (do not send cash) to cover postage and handling, payable to Harlequin Free Gift Offer. We will send you the specified gift. Allow 6 to 8 weeks for delivery. Offer good until December 31, 1997, or while quantities last. Offer valid in the U.S. and Canada only.

Free Gift Certificate

Name: _____

Address: _____

City: _____ State/Province: _____ Zip/Postal Code: _____

Mail this certificate, one proof-of-purchase and a check or money order for postage and handling to: HARLEQUIN FREE GIFT OFFER 1997. In the U.S.: 3010 Walden Avenue, P.O. Box 9071, Buffalo NY 14269-9057. In Canada: P.O. Box 604, Fort Erie, Ontario L2Z 5X3.

FREE GIFT OFFER   084-KEZ
ONE PROOF-OF-PURCHASE
To collect your fabulous FREE GIFT, a cubic zirconia pendant, you must include this
original proof-of-purchase for each gift with the properly completed Free Gift Certificate.

084-KEZR